"You have to g

Brice propelled her to
resistance surprised him—she was tiny, but
she showed remarkable strength. She was also
remarkably stubborn.

Brice lifted his eyes to the heavens. He'd been sent
down here to retrieve the missionary. But Selena was
devoted to her work and refused to go. And Brice
couldn't leave without her. She was in a lot of danger.
Too much danger.

"I have my orders," he shouted over the
thunderstorm.

"I can't leave my villagers!"

"Do you want to die, Selena?"

"I want to live—to serve these people and God."

How could he fight that kind of dedication?

In the end, he didn't have a chance. Bullets hit like
a hailstorm all around them, right along with the
rain and wind. With a grunt, Brice picked her up and
carried her through the jungle.

While Selena Carter beat at his chest every step of
the way.

LENORA WORTH

has written over thirty novels, most of those for Steeple Hill Books. She also works freelance for a local magazine, where she had written monthly opinion columns, feature articles and social commentaries. She also wrote for five years for the local paper. Married to her high school sweetheart for thirty-three years, Lenora lives in Louisiana and has two grown children and a cat. She loves to read, take long walks and sit in her garden.

CODE *of* HONOR

LENORA WORTH

Steeple
Hill®

Published by Steeple Hill Books™

STEEPLE HILL BOOKS

Steeple
Hill ®

ISBN-13: 978-0-373-44333-8
ISBN-10:   0-373-44333-1

CODE OF HONOR

Copyright © 2009 by Lenora H. Nazworth

www.SteepleHill.com

Printed in U.S.A.

He who follows righteous and mercy finds life, righteousness and honor.
—*Proverbs* 21:21

To my favorite nurse, Patricia Davids.
You are a special friend.

PROLOGUE

Somewhere in Northern Argentina

"Get on the plane!"

"No!"

Brice Whelan squinted through the rain falling all around him, his patience wearing as thin as his soaked black cotton T-shirt.

"We don't have time to argue, Selena. You have to get on this plane! Now!"

The slender woman scowling up at him pushed at her wet burnished-brown hair and shook her head. "I can't leave my villagers, Brice. I didn't call you down here to rescue me. I wanted you to help me! I won't go."

Brice wrapped a rough hand around her arm, using brute strength to propel her toward the plane. Her returning resistance surprised him—she was a tiny bit of a thing—not more than a hundred pounds at best, but she showed remarkable strength. And she was also remarkably stubborn to boot. Double trouble.

Brice lifted his eyes to the fury of the heavens, wondering why he was standing here in the middle of a rain forest when he could have been sitting by a nice fire back home in Ireland or maybe watching a baseball game on television at his second home in Atlanta, Georgia. Then he remembered—CHAIM, the elite secretive Christian organization that worked to protect and help Christians in need all over the world. As a member of CHAIM, he had a duty to bring Selena Carter, a missionary nurse who helped run a clinic here in Día Belo, Argentina, home to Atlanta.

After Selena's distraught phone call, he'd been sent down here to retrieve the devoted missionary. But Selena took her work very seriously and now she refused to go with him. And Brice couldn't leave without her. Because she'd had a near run-in with a local guerrilla group known for drug trafficking and smuggling, she was in a lot of danger. Too much danger for the humanitarian organization that had sent her here and too much danger for her rich father back home. They wanted her back in Atlanta. *Alive* and well, preferably.

Brice just wanted her on that plane so he could get out of this rain. "I have my orders," he shouted over the thunderstorm.

"And I have my integrity," she shouted back. "I should have never called you!"

All around them, the jungle and forest hissed and sang with the rage of the storm. It was wet, humid, flashing both cold and hot, and downright miserable in spite of the beauty of the place.

"Do you want to die?" he asked, hoping to sway her.

"No," she said with an expression full of conviction. "I want to live—to serve these people and God."

Brice had enough. Pulling her close with his hands over her elbows, he said, "If you don't get on that plane, you won't ever be able to do either again, *cara*. You can't stay here. It's too dangerous now. Those men will come back for you, Selena. They'll figure out you survived the attack."

"I'm not afraid."

Great. Just what he needed. A brave skinny woman willing to take on some nasty smugglers with her convictions and her honor as her only shields.

"Well, you should be afraid," he shouted. "You saw what they did to your friend Diego and to the others. I can't let that happen to you." Getting right in her face, he repeated, his Irish brogue going thick, "It's time to get on the plane, Selena."

Her violet-blue eyes widened, this time with determination and regret. "I can't leave them. I can't. They need me—I give them medicine and tend their wounds. I teach them how to read and tell them the word of God. I can't leave the clinic. I'm the only one left."

How did he fight that kind of dedication?

In the end, he didn't have a chance.

Bullets hit like a hailstorm all around them, right along with the rain and the wind. With a grunt, Brice picked her up and carried her through the jungle, slapping at ancient vines and wet, prickly palm leaves every step of the way.

While Selena Carter beat at his chest and his face every step of the way.

ONE

Atlanta, Georgia
Two weeks later

"Are you ever going to speak to me again?"

Selena lifted her gaze from the file she'd been reading to the man standing at the door of her office.

He sure knew how to fill a doorway. And he always made her heart do a funny little lurching thing that she hated and denied each time she saw him. His shaggy honey brown hair and gold-green eyes gave him the look of some sort of modern-day pirate but the precisely tailored lightweight navy suit he wore today gave him the look of a corporate raider. Selena knew he was neither of those things.

He was worse.

Brice pushed off the doorjamb and settled into a squeaky old chair across from her battered metal desk. Loosening his silk tie, he said, "Selena, it's been a couple of weeks now. You don't call, you don't write. You're breaking my heart here."

Selena slammed the file into a folder and shoved it

in the drawer of the old desk. The drawer stuck, so she tried slamming it again, pretending it was Brice Whelan's head instead. The drawer squeaked in protest while she flushed a mortified pink all the way down to her toes. She wouldn't give him the satisfaction of seeing her have a hissy fit.

She didn't have to. He got up and with one deft whack, shut the drawer tight then settled on the edge of her desk to stare down at her, the crisp crease of his pants every bit as edgy as the tension slicing through her stomach.

"You need some stress management, *cara.*"

"What I need," Selena said, tired and ready to go home to her quaint Midtown apartment and a nice bath followed by a cup of hot herbal tea, "is for you to leave. Now."

"You can't stay mad at me forever," he said, not moving. "It's me, Brice, remember? I'm just too lovable for you to stay angry. And I'm not leaving until you smile at least. You've such a pretty smile, *cara.*"

Selena's breath grabbed onto her rib cage, searching for release. He was too close. Which meant she was trapped since he was between the door and her. And that was the way Brice always made her feel—trapped in the intensity of his eyes, in the hold of his innate code of honor. Brice was too forceful, too *unwavering* for her. Just to prove he couldn't get to her, she gave him a brutal frown. "Go away."

He held his hands out, palms up, his big signet ring that bore the Whelan family fleur-de-lis crest dazzling her with flashes of gold. "I had to do it. You know that. Your father—"

"My father is still trying to control me, only this time he went too far. I called you down to Día Belo to help me solve the problem, not bring me home. His command for you to do that was the last straw."

"He cares about you."

"Yes, I know that. But he also hovers over me much in the same way you're doing right now. And I'd really like you to just leave so I can go home. I've had a horrible day and I just want some peace and quiet and maybe a sappy movie on the cable channel."

"How about coming to my house for dinner with me instead?"

Selena let that idea slide over her like warm rain dripping off a rhododendron leaf and for just a second, considered it with a full intensity—candlelight, soft classical music, the comfort of Brice's loyal considerate staff at her beck and call. But then she snapped out of that daydream. "What part of 'peace and quiet' did you miss, Brice? I don't want to have dinner with you."

He put a hand to his heart. "'Fate slew him, but he did not drop.'"

Emily Dickinson—her favorite. "And don't start reciting poetry to me. That won't work either."

She'd play dead before she'd admit that she loved it when Brice quoted poetry to her—it was just the Irish accent, nothing more, that made those moments so special. But then, there were a lot of things about her old college friend that Selena didn't want to acknowledge. Especially now, after he'd betrayed her trust by forcing her to leave the village in northern Argentina where she'd worked for more than two years.

He stood, looking exasperated, staring down at her

with those lion-like eyes imploring her, his silence shouting more than his poetry ever could. "You have to forgive me sometime, you know."

Selena put her head in her hands. "If you'll just let me go home, I'll consider it."

He huffed a sigh at that. "How *are* things, now that you're back here at the clinic?"

She let out a dry chuckle, not daring to answer that with the whole truth. "Do you actually care?"

He bent his head, his eyes slanting up toward her. "Of course I do, darlin'."

She lifted a hand in the air. "Well, then I'll tell you. Mrs. Parker has diabetes but she can't afford her medication and the closest hospital won't honor her insurance but we can't get her on Medicaid—too much red tape to explain. And I had to call in reinforcements this morning because there's a nasty spring virus going around this neighborhood and…a woman died right here in one of the exam rooms from a heart attack before we could get a transport to the hospital. She was taking the heart medication Dr. Jarrell prescribed—so we don't know yet what happened with that. The first responders don't have us on their priority list."

Before she could let out a sigh, he had her up and in his arms. "That does it then. You need nourishment. You're coming home with me."

Selena had to work hard to hide her breathlessness. "I am not."

"Yes, you are, too."

She retracted herself, the warmth, the nearness of him, too much for her to handle on this rainy Friday afternoon. "No, Brice. You can't fix things this time. We're not in college anymore. And this isn't a broken window or a flat tire or you rescuing me from my ex-boyfriend. You forced me to leave a place that I love, to leave the people that I love, and come back home to… to even more despair and sickness." Whirling to grab her battered leather tote bag, she shook her head then hurried to the door. "You can't fix this. So just go away."

Brice never listened to reason. It was his shortcoming, his downfall. He was too stubborn for his own good, really. Or, as his dear deceased grandmum used to say—*bómánta*—stupid. If he were a smart man, he'd do as Selena had asked. He'd just leave.

But he wasn't that smart. Not when it came to this particular woman. He'd known her since they were both young students, since the day he'd started college in a new city in a new country and was terrified down to his knickers, so to speak. And when it came to Selena Carter, or rather when it came to keeping Selena out of trouble, he was still terrified.

For her.

So instead of going away as she had requested, he marched after her and took her by the arm again. "I might not be able to fix this situation so you can go back to Argentina, but I can fix you a decent meal. Or at least, someone at my house can. So don't argue with me on this. Selena?"

She whirled, the scent of jasmine and sweet pea floating around her, her expression sharp-edged and full of resentment. "You, of all people, should understand how I feel. I didn't want to come back here. I wanted to stay in Día Belo because I made a commitment to those villagers and because I cared about them."

Brice lowered his head, his whisper just for her. "And you, of all people, should know that I could not leave you down there in danger. It's a matter of honor."

Hitching her tote onto her shoulder, she grabbed a pile of files off a hallway table and headed for the double front doors of the inner-city clinic known as Haven Center. "Yes, right. CHAIM honor. I know all about that. Remember, I've lived it and breathed it since birth. My father's honor, your honor—"

"The Lord's honor," Brice said, fighting to keep from grabbing her arm again. "C'mere." Reaching for the files, he shifted them to his other arm as he guided her toward the door. "We try to do God's work. You know that. And I couldn't let you stay down there after—"

"After those cutthroat smugglers killed my best friend and a good doctor, after they murdered Diego before I could help him? I watched them raid my clinic, Brice, while I cowered in the trees. Is that why you forced me to leave?"

"Well, yes, *cara*. That was certainly enough reason for me to come and fetch you home."

"*Fetch* me home?"

She marched up the hallway, locking doors and telling workers to call it a day. "You certainly did fetch me home, all right. You practically kidnapped me." Turning at the intricate doors of what had once been a church school and now served as the hub of this underprivileged inner-city suburb, she gave him a look that would trouble his dreams, her violet-blue eyes so big and luminous Brice's heart crumbled like zapped stardust right at her feet.

"They needed me," she continued. "And I needed them. Someone should have protected those villagers, too. But no, we left them to be slaughtered." Poking at his cotton shirt with a finger, she gave him a disgusted, disgraced look. "You took me and left them. And that's what I can't forgive. Or maybe I just can't forgive myself for not confronting those thugs in the first place." Grabbing back her files, she turned and stalked out the door.

The sting of her anger hit Brice with as much force as the damp spring humidity on the warm Atlanta streets. A quick spring shower had assaulted the city earlier, but the rain had stopped, leaving everything steamy and soaked. Searching, he saw her heading toward her hybrid mini SUV, her long golden-red ponytail set swinging with her frustration, her lightweight white button-up sweater sweeping away from her slender body.

"I guess that means she's not coming home with me," he mumbled. Selena, you do my head in, you know that?

He almost walked away, but he looked back up as she hit the remote key to open the SUV. When nothing happened, she hit the key again, then frowned.

Brice stood frozen by the door of the Haven Center, his instincts ramping up, his muscles clenching. Something wasn't right.

Selena stepped toward the car, still clicking the remote. Again, nothing happened. Her aggravated groan echoed down the street as she continued to hit the remote lock attached to her key chain. Finally, she looked up the street toward Brice, a determined frown on her face.

"Selena?"

Brice hurried toward her, a pulse booming inside his temple. "Selena?"

"Leave me alone, Brice! This thing hasn't worked right since I bought the car before I left for Argentina. So much for going green." Intent on finding out why her car wouldn't unlock, she reached toward the door, her fingers brushing against the lock button.

Then Brice smelled it—a strong scent of gasoline and oil. He screamed her name again, then sprinted toward her and grabbed her from behind, lifting her up as he ran with all his might away from the car. About thirty feet away, he pushed her down onto the sidewalk, knocking her files all over the concrete, his body shielding hers as he tried to cover her.

Seconds later, the explosion hit and the inside of Selena's car became an inferno of molten-hot metal and chrome.

His voice was close to her, but the buzz inside her ears made it sound so far away. "You're bleeding."

Selena looked up at the man holding her, her breath coming in deep, slashing gulps. "So are you."

She tried to sit up, tried to touch a finger to the scratch running across Brice's cheekbone. But his hand on hers brought her back down. "Don't move, *cara*. Let me make sure you're in one piece."

"I'm fine," she said, his nearness as heated as the fire from the burning vehicle. Pushing at him, she managed to shift away. "What happened?"

Brice sat her up against the clinic wall as people came running out of nearby buildings. "Your car exploded."

"But…why?" Then she looked up at him and saw it

there on his face. "Oh, no. Don't tell me. This can't have anything to do with Argentina, with La Casa de Dios?"

The grim set of Brice's mouth told her he certainly believed it did. La Casa de Dios—the house of God—was what the locals had called the clinic where she lived and worked. "I told you these were very dangerous people, luv. If you'd gotten in that car—"

Selena pushed up the wall. "No. I don't believe you. My key pad didn't work. Something malfunctioned inside the vehicle. A spark—"

Brice squatted in front of her, blood running down his face. "A bomb, Selena. A bomb happened inside that car, or at least underneath the car. You smelled the fumes, didn't you? I don't know what went wrong—maybe they weren't as expert as they thought or maybe their timer wasn't set correctly. But your key pad messing up saved you. It went off before you cranked it. Before you got inside—"

Selena took in the scene, realizing the magnitude of what he was saying. Her car was totaled, a burning heap of gas fumes and scorched metal and chrome. Thank goodness no other cars or people had been nearby. Not many ventured on this street this late in the day, so no one else had been hurt.

And she was still alive. And Brice. Brice was still alive. She thanked God for that.

He held his cell phone while he looked up and down the street. Sirens sounded in the distance. "Listen, I called 911 but we don't have much time. We have to get you away."

"Away from what?" she asked, her thoughts all jumbled up like mixed wires.

"Away…before the newspeople get here. Your face doesn't need to be plastered all over this city. They'll try to come after you again."

"But if they know where I am already—"

"We don't need to give them any more firsthand information, though, do we, luv?"

A clinic worker came running out then. "Selena, are you all right?"

Brice lifted her up. "She needs to be checked out. We don't want her going into shock."

The worker, whose nametag said Meg, looked frantic. "Dr. Jarrell left early for an out-of-town meeting, but I can call him back."

Selena slapped at Brice's hand. "I'm fine. I just want to go home." But her legs trembled like twigs.

"Not just yet," Brice said. His voice sounded far away, vacuumed, while his arms around her became a source of strength. "Meg, take her inside. I'll talk to the police and explain what happened and then I'll be in. They'll want statements from Selena and any other witnesses, but I'm going to try and deal with them first. Lock the doors and do not open them unless you see my face." When she didn't answer, Brice leaned close. "Meg, this wasn't an accident, understand?"

Meg bobbed her head, her dark eyes going wide. "I hear you, Mr. Whelan. Mercy, what's this old world coming to—a car exploding right here on the street."

Selena had to agree with her friend and coworker. Maybe this had just been some sort of random neighborhood retaliation. Maybe they'd gotten the wrong car. "Brice, are you sure?"

Brice held her close, wiping smut and grime from her

bloody face. "Don't argue with me. This is why I had to get you out of that village. They know you didn't die in that attack and now they've found you. It's not safe in Día Belo."

"And this place is?" she retorted.

He couldn't answer that, so he dropped his hand and motioned for Meg to take her. Then he turned to go and talk to the two Atlanta police officers stepping out of a patrol car. Behind them, an ambulance and two fire trucks pulled to a skidding halt.

But when Selena looked back, Brice had his hands braced on his hips and he was watching her all the way to the door. And for the first time since she'd known him, she saw something there in his eyes that she'd never seen before.

Uncertainty and fear—for her.

TWO

"**S**he is not going to be happy."

Brice took a swig of mineral water, then put the goblet down on the coffee table. Selena's debonair father, Delton Carter, sat across from him, his fingers placed together temple-style on his lap. Mr. Carter was a prominent Atlanta businessman and he was also a long-standing senior member of CHAIM—Christians for Amnesty, Intervention and Ministry. He wanted his daughter protected and he'd assigned Brice to the job. Twenty-four seven. This just might prove to be Brice's toughest assignment yet.

"We're not trying to make her happy, Shepherd," Delton said, using Brice's code name. "We're trying to keep her alive. And until we find out what kind of bomb that was, how it was triggered, and who set it up, we have to protect her."

"But she won't see it that way, sir." Brice leaned forward, remembering the terrible scene back at the downtown clinic. "She's already angry with me. This won't help matters."

"Do you care?" Selena's gray-haired dad asked.

Then he lifted a wrinkled hand. "I know how much you do care, so don't even answer that. But Brice, I want the best on this. And in my mind, you're the best. I won't have anyone else watching out for her, especially when I'm already scheduled for that mandatory meeting in Chicago next week." He shifted in the chair, worry lines slashing across his ruddy complexion. "We managed to give the police enough information that hopefully they'll help us locate the people who did this, but you know how that goes. It could be months."

"I understand, sir," Brice replied. "And you have my word that I'll do my very best to protect her while you're out of town. If she'll just cooperate."

"Cooperate with what?"

Brice turned to find Selena standing in the arched doorway opening into the spacious den of his home. "I thought you'd be fast asleep by now."

"You thought wrong," she replied, her hand brushing down the length of her burnished-colored hair. "And whatever it is you two have cooked up, you're probably right. I won't cooperate. I'm fine now, so let's just let things get back to normal."

Her father lifted out of the deep leather chair to send her a stern withering look. "Selena, surely you're not going back to the clinic."

"I *surely* will go back," she said as she stepped into the room, her hand unconsciously touching on the bandage across her forehead.

Brice took in the sight of her. She was alive and safe and that's what he needed to focus on right now. But she looked pale in the muted light glowing from the various table lamps and chandeliers in this old house. She'd had a bath and was wearing the clothes her father had brought over—a green cashmere sweater and a pair of sleek black pants. She looked incredible, considering she could have died if she'd gotten into that car.

"How are you feeling?" he asked to deflect the warring stares between Selena and her father.

"I feel just dandy." She laughed, tossed all that glorious hair away from her shoulder. "My car is destroyed and my life is in danger, but other than that, I'm just great."

"Touchy, are we?"

"Don't I have a right to be touchy? These people have disrupted my life. First, down in Argentina and now here. I'm not sure what to do next, but I won't let them stop me from doing my job." She focused on her father. "And I mean that, Daddy."

Brice had to smile. Her feminine southern wiles were kicking in. He'd caught it in the slight inflection of her darling drawl. Even scary-smart Selena Carter knew being born and bred in the South gave a woman a distinct advantage. And it didn't hurt that she had her formidable father wrapped around her finger—whether she realized it or not.

"Now, sugah, don't go looking at me like that," Delton said, coming over to give her a kiss on the forehead just below her injury. "Your mama is worried sick. She's on her way home from London right."

"I don't need Mother here to babysit me," Selena replied, all brisk business again. "Call her and tell her to stay. She'd been planning this trip for months now."

Delton shrugged. "Well, now, you know your mama, honey. She's every bit as stubborn as you. And when she said she'd be arriving at Hartsfield tomorrow morning, I knew I could set my watch by it."

Selena looked from her father to Brice. "Have you scared everybody into thinking I'm not safe?"

Brice met her gaze with a sharp scowl. "No, luv, your car exploding just a few feet away from *you* did that. Your father has hired me to be your security patrol, not because we *think* you're not safe, but because we *know* you aren't."

She waited two beats before groaning. "No! Daddy, this is silly. I don't need Brice hanging around, bothering me. I have to live my life and that means I have to keep working."

"We want you to do just that," Brice said, thinking he'd like nothing better than hanging around Selena. "And that's why I'll be by your side every waking hour during the day and that's also why you'll be staying here with me for a while. Your apartment might not be safe."

Selena shook her head so hard her hair swung out in a golden-red arc around her shoulders. "No, I will not. Daddy, we have the same security system as Brice at our house. I don't need him hovering and hindering me. I won't do it. I'll stay with Mother when she gets back instead."

"Too late, little darlin'," Delton replied. "I'm set for that big conference in Chicago next week and your mama can't protect a ladybug, let alone the both of you. She's gonna come home just to be nearby this weekend and then she'll probably meet me in Chicago next week—which was our original plan anyway. But until we both get back to town for sure I want *you* to do what Brice says. You'll have plenty of company here with

Brice's mother and his well-qualified staff and your mama can come and visit all weekend long. I've already arranged to have some of your things sent over. And that's that."

Selena bristled beautifully. "I'm staying *here?* Just like that, I have to be under house arrest with him?" Her eyebrows lifted and her nostrils flared in distaste.

Brice made a clucking sound. An arrow through his heart couldn't have had a more direct hit. "Ouch! The lady doth protest too much, methinks."

"You better believe I do, Romeo!"

"Actually, that line is from Hamlet, but I get the point."

"Do you? Do you really? You planned this, Brice. You know I'm still reeling from those murders in Día Belo and then being summoned back home and now this—forcing me to stay in this cold, drafty Tudor-style prison—"

Delton stepped forward and this time he didn't sugar-coat his words. "Would you rather I send you to Ireland for some real peace and quiet, Selena? You do know that Brice has a home there that makes this one look like a doll house. Very isolated and remote—a perfect place to reflect and consider things, but also a very good place for twenty-four-hour protection, if need be. I think it even has a dungeon or two. But for your comfort, I'm sure he'd arrange the best suite in the place—the bedroom near the turret room. The view is something else, let me tell you."

Brice grinned. "It's…just a little family estate, really."

"It's a castle," Selena retorted. "And we're all well aware of how you torment CHAIM agents who've messed up when they're sent there. You probably make them wear shirts made with fresh Whelan wool, all scratchy and itchy."

"We don't torment or torture anyone," Brice countered. "And our wool is some of the softest on earth, thank you very much."

She looked down at her own sweater. "I guess it is, but still, living around you could turn out to be torment."

"I wouldn't call it that," he said, frowning and feeling jittery. "I just try to bring jaded, frustrated agents back around. The job causes a lot of burnout and other complications. We restore their energy and their motivation and give them a fresh perspective in a peaceful, secluded atmosphere where they can meet with counselors and where they can talk to anyone about anything. I guess that can be hard on a man at times, but we are kind to our guests. It really is more of a retreat." It was a matter of pride, after all. "This job is very demanding at times." He lifted a brow toward her to indicate this was one such time.

"Well, I can certainly see why. Having to sneak around and snoop in other people's business must be tedious—"

"But necessary," her father added. "We do our best to help Christians in trouble, Selena. And right now, that's you. So there will be no arguing against my decision."

She turned on Brice. "And I suppose this was all your idea, anyway, right?"

Brice didn't know how to reach her. "I just want to know you're safe," he said, hoping she could see the sincerity in his heart. "And the only way I can know that is to see it with my own eyes."

Selena looked down at the empty fireplace, then back up at him, her expression guarded and almost evasive. For a long time, their gazes held and locked, and Brice's heart seemed to lock into place with a definite click as he threw away the key, knowing Selena had ruined him for any other woman.

The fire hissed and sputtered. She looked away first. "Oh, all right. Just for a week."

"That's all I'll need," he replied, stalling for time the only way he knew how. "I'm going to get to the bottom of this if I have to go back to Argentina myself and bring these people to justice."

Her head shot up at that. "You can't. It's too dangerous."

She amazed him. She was willing to put herself in danger, but not him. That she cared touched his heart in all the right places, but the fact that she couldn't see that she was a real target now left him cold to his bones. "Aye, it is too dangerous. And that's why I'll be guarding you for the next week, at least."

"At least?"

He cringed, then turned to leave the room before she could question him any more. "I'll just go and check on dinner. Shouldn't be long now."

"Brice, what does that mean—*at least?*"

He wanted to tell her it meant he'd protect her for eternity, but he couldn't say that. For now, he'd settle for a few days.

Which meant he had very little time. And the clock had just started ticking. He'd have to pray his way through this one.

Adele looked up as Brice entered the big beamed kitchen. "Dinner's almost ready, darling. How's Selena?"

Brice kissed his mother on the cheek, then grabbed an olive off the tray of munchies she'd fixed. Beside her in the kitchen, Betty Sager stirred the big pot of beef stew brewing on the industrial-size stove. Next to her on the long marble counter, freshly baked bread sat steaming.

Pinching at the bread, Brice said, "She's not pleased, but then we expected that. I'm hoping she'll come around once she sees this is for her own good."

"Very independent, that one," Adele said, her blue eyes twinkling with mirth. But her next words changed the lighthearted look to one of worry and dread. "Too independent. It's amazing she made it out of Argentina alive."

Betty turned to wipe her aged hands on a towel. "Nothing amazing about it—Brice saved her. Just as he saved my son and Charles and me."

Brice gave Betty a peck on her cheek. The slender, gray-haired woman was fast becoming like a second mother to him. "And how is young Roderick these days?"

"Thankful," Betty said. "We all are. We might be dead ourselves if you and Mr. Trudeau hadn't given Roderick another chance. That boy has truly seen the error of his ways."

Adele's smile brightened. "That's what we're all about, Betty. Forgiveness and intervention. CHAIM does a lot of good for Christians, and Roderick is proving he wants to be a part of that. I'm so glad Brice convinced the authorities to let him mentor your son as part of his probation."

"The lad shows promise," Brice said, remembering when just a few short months ago Roderick Sager had held a gun to Gina Malone and tried to take her son off a plane—Brice's own company jet. His friend and fellow agent Eli Trudeau had almost throttled the boy for that one. But Roderick had been threatened and coerced into doing a bad deed in order to save his parents, and the boy had learned a lot from that forced criminal intent—thanks to a visit to Brice's isolated home in Ireland, where Brice had talked with him and assured him he could work toward a second chance. Now Brice had taken him under his wing and Roderick, very savvy in technology, was in training to become a certified CHAIM agent. And his older adoptive parents—who had been threatened, too—were now members of Brice's household here in America. The arrangement worked for all involved.

Betty gave Brice an appreciative glance. "You've been so good to him, Brice. How can I ever repay you?"

"By cooking mouthwatering meals such as this one," Brice countered, uneasy with the praise. "And keeping my lovely mum company when I'm away."

"Easily done," Betty said, grinning. "Now, you go and get our guests settled in the dining room and I'll find Charles. I think he's piddling out in the garden shed. Soup's on."

"I'll be glad to do both," he told her. "I'll announce dinner to our guests then go and get Charles." Winking at his mother, he added, "This should be interesting."

Adele nodded. "Yes, since you two have been in love since you first laid eyes on each other."

"Charles and I?" Brice said with a chuckle. "No offense to him, Mum, but he's not my type." Betty grinned and laughed out loud.

"You know who I'm talking about," his mother said, shaking her head. "Selena."

"Mum, now, don't go pinning hopes on that. Selena hates me on sight."

"Are you so sure about that?"

Brice saw the sweet, knowing expression on his mother's face. He wasn't so sure about that.

Did Selena have feelings for him? Real feelings? And how did he feel about her? He knew the answer to that one. He had always loved her. But he'd never acted on that love because of his work and because of Selena's commitments. And mainly because he wasn't sure how she really, truly felt about taking their long-time friendship any further. He'd have to guard his heart with this one. Or he'd be the one in dangerous territory. Selena Carter scared him more than facing down a cell of terrorists.

THREE

Brice made it to the solarium door when he heard dainty little footsteps on the tiled floor behind him.

But the command wasn't so dainty. "Wait up."

Halting at the French doors leading out to the flag-stone terrace, he braced himself, his gaze taking in the coming dusk and the soft yellow lights of the gas lamps that burned along the garden paths all around his estate.

That request meant trouble. Selena was going to read him the riot act for forcing her to stay here.

"Don't shoot me in the back," he said, hands going up in surrender.

"Don't tempt me," she replied as she came up behind him and slapped at one of his upheld hand. "Relax. I could have murdered you years ago, but for some strange reason I didn't."

"That's because you do care about me, in spite of me being me, right?"

"I suppose so. Although, for the life of me, I can't understand it."

He slanted a look at her, thinking he understood a lot more than she did, obviously. "Are you still mad, then?"

Her shrug brought shimmering strands of curling hair fall around her face and neck. "No madder than I already was, but then I've been angry at you for one thing or another since the day we met."

Brice sure knew that to be a factual statement. Selena and he had actually gotten into an argument without even knowing each other's names that first day at the University of Georgia. He didn't really remember what the argument had been about, but he sure did remember the fiery young girl working him over with her idealist political views.

She'd been magnificent then and she was even better now. "Do you keep a list? Against me, I mean?"

"No. I'd have run out of paper long ago on that." When he guided her through the doors opening from the glass-enclosed solarium, she stopped, a soft sigh slinking out of her body as the now cool spring air hit them. Biting at her full lip, she said, "I have to admit, this has scared me more than I'm letting on."

Brice escorted her down the terrace steps, then turned to give her a tight frown, the pool's azure water glistening behind them. "Now you're beginning to see things my way."

"I didn't say that," she retorted, holding her arms close to herself to ward off the chill. "I'm still not happy about this. I know I'm at risk, but it seems silly for me to stay here since we can't be sure what actually happened with my car until we get the police report back."

Brice took in the spring evening, the freshness of the gloaming contrasting with the coldness that had come over him when he'd watched Selena's car blow up.

"Having you here while your parents are in Chicago is the only way I'll get any sleep. I can watch out for you while I research this situation myself. We can't always trust the police on these things, and CHAIM has a lot of resources for dealing with people like this."

She went back into her adversary mode. "So you're officially on the case then, not just playing bodyguard to me?"

"That's the plan, and frankly, you can either be mad or you can be glad, but I'm not budging on this. We got you safely away from Día Belo, but our work isn't done. We can't allow innocent Christians to be slaughtered by criminals, nor will we allow innocent villagers to be caught in the crossfire. We're supposed to be there to make a difference, but it's always a hassle with these militant groups and the local government both involved and constantly trying to upstage each other all around us. If it becomes too dangerous, we won't be able to send other missionaries back down there."

He watched her face in the dusk, saw the flutter of scattered emotions moving over her features with a swift clarity just like the remaining random rain clouds in the early evening sky. She shivered and he quickly took off his lightweight coat and wrapped it around her shoulders.

"Let's not talk about it right now," she said, her hands gripping the labels of his jacket. "I *can't* talk about it anymore, not tonight. It's so nice and peaceful here." They walked through the budding azaleas and the tall oaks and magnolia trees toward the large narrow gardening shed at the back side of the expansive yard. Selena took in a deep breath as they neared a cascading dogwood ripe with white blossoms. "The gardens are beautiful, Brice. Especially after this afternoon's rain."

"You can thank Charles and Betty for that. Since they've been here to supervise the yard crew, this garden has really taken off. Or as Roderick would say, 'It pops!'"

She actually laughed, the delicate giggle like the sound of tiny bells. "It was kind—what you did for him. You could have sent him to jail for a very long time."

"That's not usually the CHAIM way, unless of course someone deserves to go to jail. Then we turn them and the evidence over to the proper authorities."

She stopped near a large stone fountain sculptured in the shape of two smiling, robed women holding one clay pot while they stood by several other colorful pots, trailing wisteria vines twirling behind them. Adele called this her Ruth and Naomi fountain. Listening to the gurgling water as it spilled over the multitiered centerpiece where purple wisteria blossoms danced in the splash, she asked, "And these people who killed Diego—the ones who appear to be after me now, what do they deserve?"

He heard the danger underneath her soft-spoken words. She wanted retribution. Brice wondered just how close she'd been to the young doctor who'd been murdered in a shoot-out that had also killed several villagers, wondered what she hadn't told him during her frantic phone call to him late on that terrible night. And as he'd flown down to the tiny village of Día Belo, his imagination reeling with what might happen to her before he could reach her, he also wondered why the smugglers had targeted La Casa de Dios. True it was located in a place of poverty and despair near the border with Brazil, where the villagers had very little money and even less hope, and they did keep a cache of prescription drugs at the on-site pharmacy and dispensary there. But for the most part, Selena's team of devoted missionaries and villagers didn't cause trouble and they didn't bring on any trouble. They were simply part of a humanitarian effort trying to help.

If Selena hadn't been on the other side of the camp, checking on a sick baby when the ambush had taken place, she might have been right in the middle of the slaughter, too. She'd heard the shots as she was walking back toward the clinic and had managed to hide in the jungle growth just as the culprits finished the job and left. But she hadn't wanted to talk about what she had witnessed. And now he needed her to talk, to remember, so he could find information on how to protect her. Brice couldn't think beyond that, beyond the scent of jasmine and wisteria and the way her hair lifted in the damp night wind.

"Brice, did you hear me? How are you planning on handling this?"

Nothing about this brutal act made sense to him and he intended to dig a little deeper to get some answers. But he tried to answer *her* question in the only way he knew how. "I want justice, of course."

"CHAIM justice?" she asked, her hand trailing along a damp honeysuckle vine. "Or the real kind where they actually serve jail time for the rest of their days?"

He stopped her, taking her hands in his as he looked down at her. "You know how we handle things. We work with the proper authorities to bring any criminal to justice. But in this case, that will take a lot of evidence and a lot of cooperation with the authorities in Argentina—if we can even get them to cooperate. But first we have to gather information and find these people, and Selena, these are the kind of people who make it their business *not* to be found."

She yanked her hands away, held them up like a shield. "Well, it seems they didn't have any trouble finding me." Then she halted again, her eyes full of liquid fire as she stared up at him. "Why would they kill Diego, Brice? And why would they follow me here to Atlanta?"

"Well, that's what we have to figure out. And we will. I'm going to get busy again tracking down any information or leads I can find to see what's going on and what exactly these people were trying to keep undercover besides the obvious—we know they're smugglers but why did they suddenly attack the clinic? You don't keep the kind of drugs they deal in there, so why would they bother?"

She looked away, out toward where the sloping yard met the Chattahoochee River. "Diego must have stumbled onto something."

Brice's antenna went up on that comment since this was the first time she'd alluded to that possibility. "Did he ever talk to you about anything out of the ordinary, anything that could have caused this?"

She shook her head, then looked down. "We spent most of our time fighting red tape and trying to help patients. We didn't have time to worry about some rogue gang of militants and smugglers. Saving lives didn't leave room for anything else."

And since she'd been home, she hadn't allowed for any talk about Diego or his death or what exactly that gang had taken. All Brice had managed to piece together was that a renegade group had passed through the village and wreaked havoc on everything before murdering Diego and some of the villagers. What they'd taken or what they'd left behind was still being investigated. But nothing had been forthcoming from the local authorities. And Selena didn't seem to want to talk about it.

Brice wanted to believe she'd told him everything she could, but he'd seen the subtle shift of darkness in her expression just now. She was worried, no doubt. But she also looked unsure and—he hated to think it— guilty. He didn't press her, but he would have to keep at her until she told him everything. Maybe she was just suffering survivor's guilt and nothing more.

She hitched a breath. "He didn't deserve this. He was a good man. Such a good and noble man."

Brice couldn't respond to that. He saw her love for Diego there in her eyes and a flare of white-hot jealousy hit him square in his guts. He wanted her to look that way whenever she thought of him.

But for now, he'd have to be content with just protecting her and trying to help her bring these people to justice. And he'd have to watch as she mourned another man and waited for retribution for that man. He prayed she didn't try to take matters into her own hands. Maybe she at least understood after what had happened today that she was in serious danger.

Please, Lord, keep her safe. And help me to do my job to the best of my abilities.

He reached up a hand to push at the hair falling

around her temple, then moved his fingers to touch her wound. "Are you in pain?"

She let out a little laugh. "Right now, yes, more than I can bear. I'm bruised from falling and my head is sore. But it's not my head or my bruises that hurts. It's my heart. I think it's broken. I need to turn to my Bible and my prayers—that will give me strength."

She stepped toward Brice and wrapped her arms around his waist, then laid her head against his shoulder. "At least I have my best friend here to help me through this. Even if I am still mad at you." She squeezed him tight, her hands brushing against his back. "But you're right. I can't stay mad at you forever."

Brice brought her close, his arms taking in her tiny frame as he drank in the sweet jasmine scent of her fragrance. He wanted to hold her this way forever, to make her forget her broken heart and the man she'd found dead along with all of her other coworkers in the pouring rain down in the jungles of Argentina.

He wanted to make her forget everything that had ever hurt her. But first, he had to keep her safe.

And right now, all he could do was offer her his arms for comfort, his shoulder to lean on, his friendship and protection, just to be near her.

"We'll figure things out, *cara*. It's going to be right as rain for you—soon I hope."

She didn't say anything. Instead she just held him tight and kept her head snuggled close to his shirt. They stood that way for a few precious minutes.

Until a strange wail followed by a shout and the sound of a crash coming from the garden shed brought them apart and sent them both running.

* * *

Brice shoved Selena behind him. "Don't lose sight of me," he said, tugging her along as they hurried toward the back of the property. "Charles?" he called at the open door to the garden shed.

They heard a grunt. "In here."

Brice rushed into the long, narrow, glass-encased building where a single dim light burned. "Charles, where are you?"

"Down here, on the floor."

Brushing past bedding plants and exotic house plants, Brice ran toward the big table shoved in a corner. When he and Selena reached Charles, the older man was lying on the floor, surrounded by broken pots and a pool of dirty water.

"What happened?" Brice asked, glancing around the big shed. It was hard to see in the waning light.

"Something spooked me," Charles said, trying to sit up. "A noise. I think it might have been a big bird— maybe an owl or something. It was just such a strange noise—almost like a wail or a growl."

"Aye, we heard it." Brice's eyes locked with Selena's while she automatically began checking Charles's vital signs and examining him for broken bones. After Selena made sure Charles was breathing properly, Brice asked him, "Did you see anything—anyone?"

"No, nothing," the white-haired man answered while Selena helped him to sit up. "I was turning off lights and closing up shop. I came back here to put up the watering jug and I just heard this awful sound—like a bird's call or some sort of animal crying out—sounded like it was coming from beyond the wire fence, maybe down on the river. I jumped about a foot, hit a pot there on the floor and lost my balance and toppled right over, bringing these other pots down with me. Think I twisted my ankle." He lifted his bushy eyebrows. "I'm sorry about the mess, Brice."

"Don't worry about that. We need to get you to the house."

Selena reexamined him, asking him to speak again. She studied his face, then touched her fingers to his head, asking him questions as she analyzed him. "No symptoms of a stroke—that's good news. Can you stand?"

"I think so."

"I'd like to make sure of that," Selena said, her voice shaky. "Your pulse is racing, Mr. Sager. Did you get dizzy before you fell? Did you hit your head?"

Charles mumbled, "No, I wasn't dizzy at all, just startled. I caught myself on my arm and leg on the right side."

Brice helped lift him, then together he and Selena steadied Charles. "Is the golf cart nearby?" Brice asked.

Charles nodded, favoring his right leg. "Yep. I was gonna drive it back up to the house."

"I'll get it," Brice said. "Lean on the table and let Selena check you over a bit more until I bring it around."

Charles bobbed his head. Selena offered kind words as she helped him back against the support of the heavy wooden table. "Maybe we should call 911, Brice. Or I could call your family doctor."

"No, no," Charles replied, waving a hand in the air. "I just stumbled is all. I'll be okay. I'll take some pain pills and be good as new."

Brice shouted at Selena as he made his way to the other side of the building. "If you think he's okay to move, we'll get him up to the house and decide then."

Selena turned back to Charles. "I don't have my equipment but we can still make sure you're all right."

Charles gave her a dim smile. "My equipment ain't so good either, but I'm okay. Don't make a fuss."

Outside, Brice quickly checked for anything out of the ordinary around the perimeters of the shed. After finding the golf cart that Charles used to cover the large acreage, he drove it toward the back of the shed, then squinted into the muted light to see if he could find any footprints. The bushes and vines were wet and thick but nothing looked broken or marred. If anyone had tried to get to the estate from the river, alarms would have gone off immediately, unless someone had managed to disarm them. But this estate was airtight. Cameras everywhere, laser beams along the remote fence lines, and so many alarm and security details that even Brice had to sometimes go back over the whole layout.

Maybe Charles had been startled by a night creature such as a raccoon or a possum or, as he'd suspected, an owl shrieking somewhere off in the dense woods leading to the river.

Or maybe the old man had heard something else.

Something meant not only to scare the gardener, but also to send out a warning into the night to anyone on this property who might happen to be nearby and listening.

A warning that could turn out to be a war signal.

FOUR

Selena sat up in the big teakwood four-poster bed on the second floor of Brice's house, wondering how she'd managed to get herself in such a fix. She didn't want to be like Rapunzel, trapped in the castle, but between Brice and her father, she didn't have much of a choice right now. Too exhausted to argue after all the excitement of this day, she'd meekly come upstairs to try and get some sleep. But she couldn't relax, so she held her Bible close like a shield, trying to find comfort in the Scriptures.

But even her nightly ritual of reading verses before she went to sleep couldn't calm her. Her skin crawled with tension as she relived seeing her car explode and finding Charles lying on the floor of the shed. When she remembered the long bloody gash on Brice's cheek and thought about how much worse it could have been, she shivered in her soft fluffy bathrobe.

Ye shall not fear them: for the Lord your God he shall fight for you. That passage from Deuteronomy should bring her comfort, but she was still afraid. Not so much for herself as for those trying to protect her.

Especially for Brice. He was so fearless, so focused, that he'd do anything to protect her. Even put his life on the line.

At least Charles was all right. He'd be sore tomorrow and his right ankle was bruised so he'd have to stay off of it for a couple of days. After they brought him to the house and checked him over yet again, Charles had refused any further medical help. So Betty had taken him to their room near the kitchen while everyone else settled down to dinner. But Selena barely managed to eat a bite of the hearty stew and freshly baked bread Adele and Mrs. Sager had offered. She was too keyed up, too worried.

And she was still worried right now.

Because she hadn't told Brice everything.

And after what Charles had described, she was afraid to tell Brice or anyone else the rest. Afraid that if she voiced what she believed to be true, she'd put Brice and both their families in even more danger. And bring down the law on her beloved clinic, too. She couldn't tell anyone anything until she had proof. And so she waited and wondered. She'd enlisted help on this and had given what could become important evidence to a confidant to analyze, and now she was waiting for a report back. It wasn't that she wanted to deliberately keep anything from Brice. This was just curiosity. Or so she had thought until today. When would she hear? And how could she keep everyone safe until she had answers?

Glancing over at the battered, buttery soft, tan leather tote bag she always carried, she wondered how long she could keep her secret hidden away. What if someone tried to attack her again? What if someone got their hands on that bag? Was that why these people had tried to harm her?

And what about Charles and that sound they'd heard tonight, like a bird cawing or a cat's loud meowing, a loud sharp sound that had spooked Charles enough to make him stumble and fall. Selena and Brice had heard it too—faint and echoing—so it was hard to say. But she had heard such sounds in the jungle, and something about this particular cry tonight caused her heart to chill like a chunk of ice inside her body. She'd heard a bone-chilling cry right before her village had been attacked.

An awful, high-pitched wail that even now sent shivers up and down her spine because Selena was pretty sure the shrilling call had been made by a human being. Had it been a warning or an alert? She may never know. She only knew that right after she'd heard that sound echoing throughout the rain forest, her world had shifted and changed and she'd lost Diego. And any hopes of staying in Argentina. And now she was harboring secrets that could possibly cause her to lose her nursing license for good. And the clinic too.

What should she tell Brice?

Getting up now, Selena padded toward the chair where she'd dropped the tote, her hand reaching for the thick strap. She'd have to find a new hiding place. A knock at the door caused her to pull her hand away as if she'd touched a snake. But maybe what she'd found was worse than a snake's bite—evil and sneaky and destructive.

Pulling her robe around her cotton pajamas, she went to the door. "Yes?"

"It's only me, luv."

Brice. Her heart caught in a grip of fear and trepidation. Should she be honest with him?

"Not just yet," she whispered. She'd do a little more snooping of her own before she'd involved Brice in this. No need to get everyone all riled up on just a suspicion and something she'd found by accident. And she had no way of knowing if what they'd heard tonight had indeed been the same type of call that she had heard down in the jungle. All sorts of wildlife inhabited the woods around Brice's estate. She should know—she'd gone traipsing around with him here many times. Maybe this had been some sort of night creature. Maybe no one human had been out there in the woods.

She shivered again.

"Selena?"

He had never been a patient man.

She opened the door, a slight smile hiding the dread coursing through her system. "I'm right here, safe and sound."

"Don't scare me like that," he said, coming inside the room, his gaze scanning the big bay window and the stained glass patio doors across from the bed. Stomping to the window, he made sure the brocade curtains were pulled together. "And don't go out onto the balcony alone."

Selena watched him, knowing he was only concerned for her safety. And because of that concern, he looked a bit wild and disheveled, and about as hyper as she was right now. She needed to be kind and at least grateful, even if she did feel trapped by CHAIM's need to always be on the lookout for danger.

"I won't go out onto the porch, I promise. Even if that balcony does remind me of Romeo and Juliet."

He whirled, his hands on his hips, his eyes moving over her. "I put you here because I remembered that you liked the balcony, but you're also safer on this level and it's not that far from my suite down the hall—if you need me." He left that statement hanging in the air for a few seconds, then asked, "Are you all settled in, then?"

She took in the big room with the oversized antique furnishings and the striking Sir Frank Dicksee painting over the bed. It depicted a knight and his lady—*La Belle Dame sans Merci*. The irony of that vivid portrait weighed on her soul tonight. *The beautiful one without mercy*. Was she betraying Brice by not being completely honest with him?

"I'm nicely settled," she replied, hoping her tone sounded neutral and upbeat. "And I didn't mean what I said earlier about this being a Tudor-style prison. Your home has always been comfortable."

His brow furrowed. "But?"

"But, Brice, I've been on my own for a long time. I'm not used to such close observation. This happened so suddenly, my head is still spinning. You'll have to give me a little time to get adjusted to this new arrangement."

"Take all the time you need—just be careful and stay alert."

"I've always been careful and alert, especially when I was working down in Argentina. But this is different."

He put his hands on his hips in that Brice way she knew so well, his head lowered as he gazed over at her. "You feel as if your life had been taken from you?"

She nodded, then sank down on a bronze-colored brocade loveseat tossed with burgundy and gold pillows. "Yes. I'm a nurse. That's what I do. I don't understand how these ruthless criminals could possibly hold *that* against me. I'm all about saving people, not destroying them."

He came over to sit beside her. "They don't like us having a presence down there, luv. They can't get away with their dirty work if we get in the way." He leaned back, fatigue pulling at his features. "It would help with our investigation here if you could remember something, anything that might have provoked this attack."

Selena glanced toward her bag, wondering why she couldn't just show Brice what she'd found and tell him her suspicions, maybe tell him about her own independent investigation. But what if she was wrong? That would open up a whole new set of problems. Better to wait until the right time to figure this out, if ever. "I don't know," she said, not quite meeting his gaze. "It all happened so fast. One day we were going about our business, examining patients, and the next, this gang of militants came crashing through the jungle and out into the village to destroy what we'd worked so hard to build, not only our physical buildings but the trust of the natives, too. I'm sure the camp is gone by now since everyone abandoned it the minute the shooting started. Even me."

Brice's finger on her chin brought her head around. "I haven't told you this because I didn't want you to worry, but I sent reinforcements down there to help the locals. They got as many of them to safety as they could. But you're right, most had scattered and couldn't be found." Rubbing his finger down her cheek with a feathery touch, he said, "I did try, *cara*. I did it for you. And I did it because it's not my nature to leave any innocents behind."

"Oh, Brice." Selena pulled him close, hugging him tight as she'd done so many times in her life. But this time, this time when she lifted her head, her eyes meeting his, a surge of longing and need rushed through her, a feeling that was both foreign and familiar, both joyful and frightening. And from the shattered, searching look in Brice's eyes, he felt the same. Bewildered, Selena pulled away. "I appreciate that. The villagers have been on my mind. I wish—"

"I know what you wish, but you can't go back there. Not now, maybe not ever." He got up, as if the awareness they'd just felt had scorched him with its power. He paced, as was his nature, his hands fidgety, his eyes flashing. He pushed at his tousled hair. "Right now, we have to focus on finding out who tampered with your car. I'm thinking it was either a pipe bomb or some sort of backpack hidden underneath the chassis. Once we know for sure, we move from there. Maybe it will be local and a random thing, but I doubt that. I'm pretty sure it was a message from Los Andedores del Noche—"

"The Night Walkers," Selena translated, recalling the notorious Brazilian gang of smugglers. "They never bothered us before."

"There's a first time for everything, luv. Especially when criminals are involved."

A cold reality seeped over Selena while she watched Brice trying to focus on the problem at hand. He wasn't ready to get any closer to her because he had a job to do—and this time the job involved *her*. He'd always taken his CHAIM oath very seriously and this had caused Selena to never take him seriously—as anything other than a good friend. They were still that—just good friends. She was projecting her fears into something more—this strong bond between them would naturally grow in the midst of all this danger. But Brice would always put duty first. She'd be wise to remember that.

"What about you?" she asked to hide her disappointment and this unfamiliar longing. "Don't you need to get back to Ireland and Whelan Wool?"

"Whelan Wool runs itself," he replied, his pacing only adding to her awareness of him. "I have the best management team in the world and I'll be in constant contact with them, no doubt. They're used to me being absent a lot."

"But you love the shearing season, Brice. You love getting down and dirty and working along with your men."

"Aye, that I do. But I love—" He stopped, his gaze moving over the room, one hand lifting out in the air. "But I have a responsibility to you right now, and besides, it's a couple of months before shearing starts back up. So don't you worry about any of this."

"While you take on the burden?" she asked, seeing him in a whole new light. Or rather, seeing the light that shined through his character much more clearly now.

"You're no burden, *cara*. None a'tall."

With that, he bent to kiss her on the cheek. "Sleep well, princess. And say your prayers."

And then he left her sitting there, staring after him with her guilt and her secrets pressing on her soul.

* * *

Brice couldn't sleep. So he walked the perimeters of the property, checking on concealed cameras, securing already secure high fences. This rambling old house had belonged to his mother's side of the family for close to one hundred years. After his father died a few years ago, Adele had immediately come home to Atlanta. She could always be found here when she wasn't traveling or visiting Whelan Castle in western Ireland.

Adele loved the castle and its rich heritage, but unlike Brice, she couldn't stay there in seclusion for months on end. And while she supported Whelan Wool and traveled as a spokesperson to promote the farm and their mills, she would never understand Brice's need to work with his hands on the land that had been in his family for centuries. That didn't matter to Brice. He didn't mind living in two worlds. His CHAIM duties had him traveling all over the world anyway.

So besides the obvious, he couldn't figure out why he was so on edge tonight. He longed to be back in Ireland, working the farm, watching his sheep dogs, Greta and Piper, corner a herd of blackface ewes and yearlings to help him bring them down from the mountains. Okay, so he missed Ireland; that was nothing new. And while he loved the cosmopolitan energy and urban intensity of Atlanta, his time here now wasn't turning out to be a relaxing, fun visit.

He stopped, the dark night surrounding him as a thousand nocturnal sounds assaulted his senses. Living near the Chattahoochee River made for interesting late-night walks. But tonight even the creatures scurrying and singing all around him couldn't put Brice on such high alert. No, something else was nagging at his soul right now.

Yes, he was worried. About Selena. About these nasty people who seemed determined to scare her and possibly harm her. But there was something else hanging like a loose vine near his consciousness. And Brice wouldn't sleep until he could pinpoint that something else.

So he walked and listened and went over everything in his mind. Selena's SUV had been bombed in a bad area of downtown Atlanta, and a few hours later, an unusual sound had come from the back of Brice's estate north of the city. The bombing was surely a cause for concern, but something about the incident tonight bugged Brice. Charles was a naturalist and outdoorsman. That man knew every kind of bird call and every kind of animal cry in Georgia and beyond. So why had he been so spooked by what he'd heard tonight?

And what about Selena? She'd been as shaky as Charles by the time they'd taken the golf cart back to the house. At the time, Brice had chalked it up to the events of the day. But now…he had to wonder if he'd missed something.

Selena was usually very cool under pressure, especially when she was with a patient. She was a top-notch R.N., one of the best. But tonight, she'd been too skittish when she'd examined Charles. Normally, she would have insisted on getting her patient to a doctor. Maybe Charles had convinced her differently, or maybe she'd been too flustered to think straight.

Brice stopped again, then looked up toward the room where a light still burned. Selena's room. She was trapped up there like a princess in a castle. And her fears seemed trapped inside her memories and her mind.

Then he understood. She wasn't telling him everything. He could sense that each time he asked her about her memories. He'd interrogated enough people in his life to know when someone was being evasive. And he'd noticed a sense of guilt floating like an aura all around Selena each time he asked her for more details. Was Selena withholding information on purpose? Or was she just confused and scared?

Why would she hide things from him, of all people?

Maybe because she didn't want him to find out the truth?

That was the thing. Selena and he had shared a lot during their years as friends. What would make her clam up now, when he needed to know everything in order to help her? It didn't make sense.

Unless she was trying to protect someone else.

He thought of a James Joyce poem—"Alone." "The sly reeds whisper in the night. A name—her name—"

Selena. That was the name calling to him tonight.

Brice grunted, kicked at the soft grass at his feet. He didn't like being so helpless and feeling so alone. He needed answers. But how could he get those answers if the woman he was trying to protect didn't want to tell him the truth? What could be so scary or so important that she felt the need to keep it to herself?

Saying a prayer for help from a higher source, Brice took a long, calming breath and asked God to guide him. Then he stared up at the big bay window and wondered what secrets Selena had brought home from Argentina.

And he wondered how he'd ever convince her to let go of those secrets so he could help her and protect her.

FIVE

"Is this really necessary?"

Selena glanced over at the stoic man driving her to work. "Brice, are you listening to me?"

His sigh slid out through a muttered "Aye." Watching the rush hour traffic on Interstate 75, he said, "But *you* obviously haven't been listening to *me*. I'm going to be with you, day and night, in one way or another."

Selena groaned her own frustration. "We were together on your estate all weekend, Brice. And nothing else out of the ordinary happened. Do you really think it's necessary to stay with me at the clinic all day long, too?"

"Yes, I do." He merged onto Peachtree and sat silent in the stop-and-go traffic, then finally turned off onto a side street that took them into an aged, boarded-up neighborhood. "My estate is airtight and heavy on security, but working in this part of the city makes you an open target. It was too easy for someone to walk right up to your car and stick explosives underneath it."

"But you don't think they'd be that bold again, do you? That they'd come back right away and try something else?"

"Yes, I do think that's exactly what they might do. And each time, they'll get a little bolder. Someone got to your car, Selena, and from what the crime scene investigators have found, they plugged your car with just enough explosives to damage it, not blow it to pieces. They were trying to either scare you with a deliberate threat, or, if you'd gotten into the car, hurt you or worse—kill you. That means they've probably been watching the clinic and timing exactly when you leave work each day. They can just as easily get to you in your apartment or inside the clinic. I've got people watching your apartment, but your workplace is especially vulnerable to attacks."

She knew it was pointless to argue with him since she'd tried all weekend, but doing it made her feel more in control. "Won't you get bored, just following me around?"

He patted the computer case behind the seat. "I brought work with me. I'll catch up on e-mail from the farm, do some research into the gang that attacked your camp—"

"You said they don't want to be found."

"Yes, but as you well know, CHAIM has the resources to find anything and anyone. I'll keep digging. I'll probably be so busy all day long with my cell and my laptop, you won't even know I'm here."

She knew him too well to believe that, and she also knew herself too well. She was always aware of Brice when he was around. Even though he'd pretended to stay busy back at his house over the last couple of days, somehow he'd shown up to check on her every hour on the hour, and somehow he'd known when she wasn't in her room. "Busy, yes," she said now, "but you'll still manage to watch out for me?"

"Yes. Not a bad day's work, is it now?"

"We'll see." Selena waited until he'd parked his truck in the old parking garage across from the clinic. "I just want to warn you, my work isn't glamourous."

He grinned over at her. "But you sure look good doing it. I like the yellow duckies on your scrubs."

Selena couldn't deny the rush of warmth surging through her frazzled mind. Each time Brice looked at her that way, she had to smile. But why now? Why did she want to be around him more now, when she also wanted her freedom again with every fiber of her being?

Just nerves, she reasoned. Just one more complication in her life. She hadn't seen Brice for two years. Two years with very little communication in all that time. And then, he'd burst back into her life, all flash and fire, determined to save the day.

Well, she *had* called him. Still wondering why she'd done that, Selena chanced a glance at him now, a sweet longing clouding her vision as well as her rational thoughts. Shaking her head, she stared down at the files in her lap. Had she called Brice as a last resort? Or had she called him for other unnamed reasons?

She'd been in trouble. And Brice was the man to call when you were in trouble. And Brice was the man who'd stick around when the going got rough. She should have realized that, should have remembered that he was too noble to just rescue her and then leave again. Brice would always stay the course.

"Selena, are you afraid to go to work today?"

She looked up to find Brice out of the truck and

leaning back in toward her. "No, I'm fine. I just—I don't know how to thank you for helping me."

"You can thank me by letting me do my job," he retorted. "Now, remember the plan. You don't make a move without telling me. Don't go outside for fresh air, don't go the ten blocks to the Starbucks on the upscale corner."

She got out of the car, her files and her bag secure in her arms. "Do I get bathroom breaks?"

"Only if another woman goes in there with you— someone who's been cleared."

"Now that's downright paranoid."

"You'd be surprised what can go wrong in the loo, darlin'. So don't try anything without clearing it with me—even powdering your cute nose."

She walked around the big truck, listened as he hit the lock system, then marched down the concrete ramp toward the old church school where, through government grants and private funding alike, she'd managed to help Dr. Henry Jarrell build the Haven Center Clinic. She'd worked here for a couple of years after leaving her position at one of the large hospitals. When Dr. Jarrell had pegged her to head the Argentina mission, Selena had jumped at the chance to serve. She didn't want to jeopardize either the clinic here or her efforts in Argentina. And today, she needed a few minutes of privacy to check on something important. Something she couldn't explain to anyone, especially Brice.

When they reached the spot where her car had burned, Selena stared at the blackened road and sidewalk, more determined than ever to get to the truth. "I still can't believe this happened."

Brice instantly put a hand to her elbow. "It was a close call but we gave the police a thorough report. At least the papers and evening news played it down enough to keep you out of the spotlight for now. They listed it as some kind of engine malfunction or possible tampering, but no mention of any connections with Día Belo. I'm sure your father had something to do with that, since CHAIM is a silent backer of the clinic."

"This clinic is important to me," she said. "If I can't go back to Argentina, then I can at least make a difference here. I have to stay focused, Brice. I have to do my job, too, just like you. I won't abandon these patients."

"Then we'll get along just fine," he replied. "I don't want you to give up your work. I just want to find out who's messing with you and put a stop to it."

"So do I." And she meant that. But she was still afraid to tell him everything she feared. Because if she was right, she might lose the clinic and everything else she'd worked so hard to build. And she might not be able to practice nursing again, ever.

Brice opened the creaky old doors to the clinic, allowing Selena to go inside ahead of him. She was at once assaulted with a waiting room full of Monday-morning patients, all here to see the good doctor and her—his head R.N. Selena started barking orders to the other staff as she went right into action mode, thriving on the chaos because it allowed her to forget all her worries. She'd have to tell Brice the truth sooner or later, but right now she had to concentrate on work. She welcomed the distraction.

"Selena, how are you?"

She turned from assessing a patient in the waiting area to find Dr. Jarrell smiling at her. "Hi, doc."

The older man reached out to hug her, then glanced toward Brice with a nod. "I'm so sorry about what happened, dear. I was halfway to my conference in Savannah when Meg called me. Are you sure you're all right?"

Selena touched the bandage on her head, then let her glance skim over the red scratch along Brice's cheek. "I'm fine. But we were all a bit shaken."

Her gray-haired mentor nodded, concern etched in his craggy face. "Have the police told you what set off the explosion?"

Brice stepped up. "I'm Brice Whelan. I was here with Selena when her car blew up. I've been working with the police to get to the bottom of this. Right now, all we know is some sort of explosive pack was wired to Selena's car and it was possibly activated with a timer. At first we thought her key pad's malfunction might have interfered, but it seems that actually saved her. She would have been in the car when the bomb went off if her key pad had worked properly."

"Brice, is it?" The doctor gave him a patronizing smile. "Thanks for the thorough explanation."

Selena looked from the doctor to Brice, sensing some territorial tension. "I'm sorry. Brice, this is Dr. Henry Jarrell. Dr. Jarrell and I started Haven Center together several years ago. He's the one who convinced me to give up all the hassles of working at a big hospital for the good life here."

Dr. Jarrell smiled at her sarcasm. "And I'm very glad I did so. I sure missed Selena when we sent her off to set up our fledging clinic in Día Belo. I'm relieved she's back here and safe, although I'm not happy about what happened down there—not one bit. And now this."

Brice shot Selena a glance, then turned his attention back to the doctor. "I'm here to make sure she stays safe. I'll be her security detail for the next week or two."

The doctor's wrinkled face registered shock. "A bodyguard? Are things that serious?"

"A bomb is very serious," Brice replied, bristling. "We think this incident could very well be connected to the attack on the clinic in Argentina."

Selena lifted her gaze to him, hoping to send him a warning to back off. Dr. Jarrell hadn't even been around the day of the explosion, so he didn't have a clue about any of this. "It's just a precaution," she said. "We don't even know why these people—if it was them—are targeting me. But you know how my daddy is. He's been concerned since I came back home, and my car blowing up didn't help matters."

"Ah, well, can't say that I blame him," Dr. Jarrell replied. "From what I've been able to glean from my sources in Argentina, it's a good thing you did come home. I've been told our clinic is destroyed. And it looks like they robbed the pharmacy, so that makes me think they were definitely after drugs."

Brice's eyebrows lifted at that. "Can we trace these drugs? If you give me a list—"

"I've got people handling that," Dr. Jarrell said. "And it looks like you've got more than enough here to keep you busy, son." Then he motioned toward the waiting area. "I guess we'd better get started. It's going to be a long day."

* * *

"I don't like this."

Brice opened the truck door for Selena, his bad mood increasing with each minute. It had started with that old doctor's condescending attitude and had grown increasingly worse as the day wore on. Dr. Jarrell obviously cared about Selena, but the man was working her to death. She practically ran the clinic all by herself. And now, she had to visit a patient off-site in one of the worst areas of the city.

"I have to go," she said, huffing a breath as she scooted onto the seat. "And since you're my only mode of transportation, that means you get to tag along with me."

"Can't you find someone else to do this?"

"No, I can't. In-home visitation is part of my job. We have a lot of patients who can't come to us, so we go to them, but usually two of us go together, if that makes you feel any better."

"It does, but not much."

"Mr. Cooper is one of those patients and he's a favorite of mine. He has major heart problems—too many to name. I'm just trying to make his last days a little better. And besides, Dr. Jarrell put him on new medication about two weeks ago, hoping to delay the inevitable. I need to follow up on that."

Brice got in the truck and cranked it, glad for the air-conditioning it provided. "I admire your compassion, but this is dangerous—even if we weren't on high alert."

"I'm always careful," Selena replied, her mind on the patient's records she'd brought along. "Mr. Cooper is a very nice man. He's put out the word for the neighborhood gangs to leave me alone."

"Well, that makes it ever so much better then."

Selena shut the file and glared over at him as they headed out into the afternoon traffic. "We get to go home after this and I'm glad. You're not handling this very well. I told you you'd get bored."

"Bored is the last thing I am," Brice assured her. "More like petrified. How do you do this, day in and day out?"

Selena saw his frown, but refused to back down. "Because it's my job. Yes, it's hard to watch an AIDS victim slowly withering away. It's hard to have to deal with infections and gunshots and high blood pressure and kids who need vaccinations or to watch teen mothers delivering premature babies who are probably hooked on drugs. But it's what I do, Brice. If you can't deal with that, then you don't have to be here."

Brice hit his hand on the steering wheel. "I'm sorry, *cara*. Yours is a necessary vocation. I see that. But your doctor back there seems to take you for granted, or have you even noticed?"

She laughed out loud. "Dr. Jarrell? He's like my second father. We both work hard, so no, I don't see that he's taking me for granted. He depends on me since I'm his only full-time nurse right now."

"Well, maybe he needs to hire another full-time nurse."

She held to the dashboard, the shifting gears making her rock back and forth. Brice had insisted on driving his hunting truck in order to avoid unwanted attention. "We don't have the funding for that. We barely get by as it is now and that's with government funding and in-kind donations from private patrons. It's a never-ending battle. If we didn't have the support of several area churches, we wouldn't even be able to maintain this clinic or the one we started in Argentina. Thank goodness CHAIM supports us, too, even though that's not common knowledge." She turned the air-conditioning vent toward her flushed face. "And speaking of Argentina, Dr. Jarrell has assured me he intends to reopen the clinic. He's maintained contact with the local crew—we were able to train some of the villagers to become certified in the basics. Once all of this is settled, they can keep it going only with the bare essentials, but I want to go back down there as soon as possible."

"Did the doctor suggest that?"

"He mentioned it, yes. He wants me to resume my work there as soon as this problem blows over, but he's willing to make sure things have settled down first."

Rushing through a caution light, Brice turned to her. "Does he understand that people have died down there, Selena? Has he offered to go down there himself, instead of sending you?"

"As a matter of fact, he suggested we fly back down there together," she retorted, her head propped in her hand as she rested her arm on the door handle. "I think that's a very good idea—I mean, once this is cleared up."

"That might take a while."

Selena shot him a questioning look. "Did you find out anything in your research today?"

He gave her a level glance, wondering why her voice seemed to quiver ever so slightly with that question. "Yes, I did. There are numerous reports on smuggling in that area. It's a main international thoroughfare. And from what I read and heard, the gangs pretty much ride roughshod over the local authorities, which is probably why we can't get anyone down there to cooperate with us. It might take a while to pin this down. And until then, you will remain here."

"Is that an order?"

"That's a request, from your friend here, okay?"

"But you can't be with me all the time, Brice. That's unreasonable to ask of you."

"I don't mind."

"You have other obligations."

"This is my first priority right now." He turned toward a long, littered street. "Look, it's getting late. I want you in and out of Mr. Cooper's place before nightfall."

Selena pointed to the dilapidated house at the corner of the dead-end street. "I'll be done when I'm done. Some things can't be rushed."

Brice wondered about that. He'd certainly been patient with this woman since the day he'd met her. But her stubborn independence trumped his patience any day. She was going to drive him crazy with her need to serve and her disregard of the danger in doing so. While he certainly admired that quality, he also worried about her. Selena would do her job, no matter the consequences. But would she be cautious? And would she know to tell him of anything suspicious? He had to wonder again if she knew more than she wanted to share. His gut burned yes to that question.

"Let's just get on with it," he told her as he parked the truck.

They got out and headed up the broken stone steps to the tiny shack. Selena knocked, then called out, "Mr. Cooper, it's me, Selena. I'm coming in."

At the unlocked door, Brice turned to see a dark economy car cruising slowly up the street. Entering the dim living room with Selena, he pivoted at the window.

The car stopped at the other end of the street, looking as out of place as a rose blooming in bramble. Brice thought about going out to confront whoever was watching them. But Selena called out to him, her voice so frantic, he forgot about the car out on the road.

"Brice, hurry!"

Brice rushed toward the stifling hot bedroom at the far end of the shotgun house, the stench of death surrounding him as he entered the shuttered room.

"We're too late," Selena said, her voice raw with emotion. "Mr. Cooper is dead. We need to call 911."

SIX

"How are you?"

Selena turned at Brice's question. She'd been sitting in the window box by the big fireplace in the den. Just sitting, staring out the wide bay window that showed off the pool and the surrounding gardens.

"I'm okay."

She wasn't okay and he didn't know what to do for her. She'd tried everything in her power to help that sick old man, but in the end her efforts hadn't helped at all. He'd died alone in a place of squalor. After they'd watched the ambulance take Mr. Cooper away, Brice had managed to get her home. Then they'd had a quiet dinner with both their mothers, a meal Selena barely touched so she'd excused herself and had come in here. Not even the ever cheerful, talkative Beatrice Carter could get Selena to say much during dinner, and Brice wasn't sure he could get her to talk now. His mother was up in her room reading and Bea had reluctantly gone home with her own security guard, leaving her daughter here with the assurance that Brice would "take care of her."

He was trying.

Selena was such a strong woman, not one for theatrics or tears. But for some reason, finding Mr. Cooper dead earlier today had rattled her. She'd quietly cried all the way home, then she'd gone through the motions of eating, mostly just pushing her food around on her plate.

"Do you want some hot tea or a bit of one of Betty's fresh apple tarts? I know they're your favorite and you didn't have one after dinner."

"I'm not hungry."

"Would you like to listen to some music?"

She finally turned, her eyes puffy, her voice raw and gravelly. "No."

He stood with his hands in his pockets, taking in the sight of Selena sitting there like a lost little girl. Whenever he imagined her here in his home, in his dreams, she was happy, laughing and content. She did not look content tonight. He could handle her anger, he could deal with her criticism and frustration. But he'd never had to deal with Selena in this way. She seemed to be shutting down, giving up. Seeing her so despondent left Brice feeling helpless, no, make that useless. He'd rather she rant at him than just sit there, so forlorn and so quiet. But if the lady wanted to be by herself—"I guess I'll leave you alone, then."

"Brice, wait."

He turned to find her eyes fixed on him, her expression unsure and hesitant. "Yes?"

"Could you…could you read me some poetry?"

His heart turned as soft as the gooey center of Betty's famous tarts. "Of course, luv." He went to the bookshelves covering two walls of the high-ceilinged, long room. "What will it be today—Dickinson, Wordsworth, Frost, Keats?"

"Marlowe," she said, her hands tucked around her bent knees, her head resting on those hands.

"Marlowe it is then."

He found a hefty volume on English playwrights and poets and quickly turned to Christopher Marlowe. "Any preference?"

She nodded, her eyes touching on his with a mixture of trepidation and yearning. "The one about the shepherd."

Brice settled into a chair across from her, smiling over at her through the lamplight. He found the poem, then cleared his throat. "'Come live with me and be my love….'"

Selena closed her eyes while Brice recited the rest of the famous poem. When he'd finished, his heart's longing echoing the words on the page, he looked up to find her with her eyes still shut, a single tear trailing down her cheek.

He was up and beside her, tossing the book onto the chair behind him. "C'mere."

She allowed him to take her into his arms. Brice sat back on the cushioned window seat, pulling her close. "Go ahead and cry, *cara*. You need to cry."

She sniffed, wetting his shirt with her tears. "You and your poetry. I shouldn't have asked for Marlowe. That one always gets to me."

"You're just tired and still in shock," Brice said, thinking that one always got to him, too, because he wanted it to be so between them. He wanted her to come live with him and be his love, through valleys, groves, hills and fields. And through all the bad and good of life—he wanted her to be his. But she wasn't ready for all that; she might not ever be ready for that. "It's all right," he told her, kissing the top of her head. "You lost Diego and you almost died yourself. Seeing Mr. Cooper today just brought it all out. Delayed reaction, posttraumatic stress—that's only natural after what you've been through."

She moved her head in response, her shuddering sob making her tremble. "He was a nice old man suffering from heart failure and I was hoping the last round of medication we prescribed for him would give him a bit more time. He worked for years at a local factory, day in and day out, trying to provide for his family. His wife died a couple of years ago and his children moved away. But he stayed in that horrid neighborhood because it was his home."

"I'm sorry," Brice said. "Truly. It must be hard on you, losing patients you've become attached to."

"I don't usually let it get to me," she admitted. "It's just that…I'm so worried about the patients I left behind at the clinic—the villagers who were so kind and so devoted to helping out all the time. And now, I have to worry about someone trying to hurt me, which means I have to worry about Dr. Jarrell and Meg and all the volunteers and patients at the clinic here, too. And you, Brice. I'm so worried about you."

"You don't need to worry a fig about me, luv. I've been taking care of myself for a long time now. And I've dealt with worse than these nasties, let me tell you."

"But I do worry," she said, her gaze insistent. "It just

hit me today when I found him." She looked up then, her eyes like dew-kissed violets. "He knew what real love was, Brice. He knew."

Brice tugged her chin up with his hand. "So do you. You've got the love of Christ in your heart. And that's why you're hurting so much right now, because you care so much."

"I do care," she said, her face wet, her lips parted. "Diego was… special to me. Those workers who died with him—their lives have to matter. Why did God take them and spare me? Why?"

Brice couldn't answer that one, but he'd sure seen enough survivor's guilt to understand why she was so upset. He shook his head. "I don't know. But I do know that you're here for a reason. Maybe the Lord has something big in store for you, something that will justify their deaths and bring honor to them."

She abruptly sat up. "There is no honor in my heart right now. I just feel so empty."

Her torn, broken words shattered Brice's resolve. He leaned close, forcing her back into his arms, his lips grazing hers. "Your heart is *full* of honor, Selena. Trust me on that." Then because he couldn't resist, he kissed her, first her lips, then her tears.

She didn't try to stop him; she didn't pull away. Brice took that as a sign to continue, so he did, savoring the sweetness of her lips, loving the soft sigh that drifted between them when his lips touched hers. When he lifted his head to stare down at her, her eyes were wild and lush with the kind of longing he felt inside his very bones.

"You're a good friend," she said, her smile bittersweet,

her voice grainy and low. Then she laid her head against his shoulder. "Thank you for letting me have a good cry."

"Anytime," Brice replied, her words at once comforting and biting. "Isn't that what a good friend is for?"

She answered him with a swift smile and a quick kiss. "Yes."

Brice swallowed the lump inside his throat and held her close, cherishing this quiet intimacy. And in the silence, he allowed his heart to dream a shepherd's dream, to recite a poet's lyrics. Because one day, she would live with him as his wife. He wouldn't rest until that happened—he'd seen it, accepted it on the plane trip to Argentina and again when she'd almost stepped into that bomb. Having come so close to losing her for good, he was tired of wasting time pining away for her when he should be fighting for her love instead. He didn't know why it had taken him so long to admit that to himself.

But first, he had to make sure she lived to marry him. And he had to gain her trust so she'd tell him whatever it was she was so obviously trying to keep to herself.

Holding her with one hand, he quickly drew the curtains with the other, hoping to block out the danger for a little while at least.

Selena couldn't sleep. Thinking about how Brice had kissed her earlier that night, she wished for the hundredth time she hadn't asked him to read her that beautiful poem. But…she'd had to do something, say something, to keep from blurting out all her fears to him.

She was almost certain Mr. Cooper's death had come prematurely. She was almost certain he'd been given the wrong medication. It looked like the right medication, but she couldn't be sure until she figured out a way to have it analyzed, too. She'd taken a couple of the pills from the bottle, to hide away, before the paramedics had arrived to take his body to the morgue. There would be an autopsy since he died in his home, and Selena wondered if that would show anything significant. She couldn't wait for the results of that. She had to send these pills to be analyzed by her friend at the lab where she'd sent the ones she'd found at the clinic. Secretly analyzed. In her line of work, with junkies and street brokers, she knew a few tricks of the trade. And she knew to wait until she had all her ducks in a row before blurting anything out.

But she'd come so close to mentioning her worries to Brice tonight. She'd almost told him her suspicions, all of her suspicions—from the day she'd left the clinic until now. She didn't know why she was so afraid to say what was on her mind, maybe because if it were true then everything she'd worked so hard for would be destroyed.

Destroyed by deceit and betrayal, by greed and evil.

I have to tell him soon. If she didn't report this, she'd be the one going to jail.

She knew that, but tonight she'd just wanted to forget all of it, just for a few minutes. And there earlier by the window, with the moonlight shining on the blossoming white azaleas and dogwoods, she'd needed some sort of gentle reminder that life was precious and that no matter what, Christ would see her through. And Brice would be there with her.

So far, they had both come through for her time and again. Selena needed to remember that, in spite of her fears. She walked across the soft antique floral rug to her bed, crawled in and tried to focus on the paperwork in front of her. If she could find some sort of discrepancy in these patient files, she might be able to get to the bottom of her worries, or at least if she found nothing out of the ordinary, then she could rest assured that she was just imagining things. It was a start and it kept her mind off other things, such as the way Brice's kisses made her feel.

Wondering why she'd never kissed him before, Selena smiled. Back when they'd first met and gotten to know each other, she'd sure thought about kissing Brice. Lots of times. But once Brice had met her father that had been that. Delton had pegged the rash Irishman and devout Christian as a perfect fit for the CHAIM agent profile. And once Brice had heard the details, he'd been determined to join CHAIM. His wish to serve had immediately put him off limits in her mind—she'd seen how her mother worried for weeks on end, wondering if her father would return home safe or not, and she'd lived with all the necessary secrecy, all the covert discussions that went on day and night behind closed doors. She'd been so disappointed when Brice had told her he wanted to join up, Selena had written him off as far as romance. Brice had become a good friend, nothing more. Best to leave it that way. She wouldn't want to lose that friendship. If she allowed these new, exciting feelings to overtake her logical mind, that could very well be the case.

Of course, right now, she wasn't being very logical about anything. While she cringed at how badly she'd handled Mr. Cooper's death, she also understood that it had been the catalyst for the release of all of her other hidden fears and emotions she'd held at bay since the day Brice had put her on that plane for home. Too much, too soon—too much to comprehend, too much that had changed her safe, secure world, too many things that had shifted her strong faith. She'd talked to her pastor and a church counselor after arriving back in Atlanta, but having Brice to hold her had helped immensely, too.

The shrill ringing of her cell phone pulled Selena out of her thoughts. Wondering who'd be calling at this late hour, she grabbed it off the nightstand. Probably her mother, concerned and just checking. Or maybe Meg. She often called after hours to give Selena patient updates.

She didn't recognize the number. "Hello?"

The male voice had a lazy but intimidating drawl. "You have something we want."

Selena sat up in bed. "Excuse me?"

"Usted tiene algo que deseamos."

Selena's pulse pounded inside her head like the beating of a tribal drum. "Who is this?"

"Just watch your mouth, lady. Or next time we'll make sure you're *in* the car when we blow it up."

The blaring silence hit Selena full force, cutting off her breath. She threw the phone down, then stared at it as if the nasty voice on the other side would shout out at her again. That voice had been American, with a southern drawl that crawled like biting ants across her nerve endings. But even with the poor pronunciation, the Spanish translation had been very accurate.

They knew she had something. They knew she was hiding something. And that meant that her worst fears had come true.

SEVEN

Brice glanced up at the clock hanging next to a floral cross on the sterile white wall. After five. The clinic had whirled through another busy spring afternoon while he'd read over the files he'd downloaded last night. This was a lot of information to digest, but he'd study it until all the pieces fell into place. With little cooperation from the local militia in Día Belo and very little help here in Atlanta, he was going to have to dig deep to find out why these thugs had raided the clinic. Obviously, for drugs but was there something more? They'd never bothered the clinic before. Why now? And who exactly had bombed Selena's car? The police didn't seem to have much to go on except to confirm that it was definitely a crudely made bomb. No prints, no significant evidence at the scene, nothing to connect that incident to the raid in Día Belo. But Brice knew they had to be connected.

So far, through his sources in Argentina, Brice had gathered information on the group known in Día Belo as Los Andedores del Noche—the Night Walkers. Fitting, since like cockroaches, they only came out at night to move their goods. It seemed apparent that this group had been behind the attack on La Casa de Dios. While nothing could be pinned to them, or at least no one had bothered to gather a case against them, it seemed to be common knowledge in the village that they dealt in smuggling and moving stolen goods—sometimes fake designer purses and other things and sometimes guns and other weapons. Not a pretty group to be involved with.

But why had they bothered the clinic? Were they into selling prescription drugs on the black market, too?

Most guerrilla factions usually left Christian organizations alone. Most. Some didn't care one bit who they tormented or bothered, and some hated Christians. Maybe this group was that kind, without scruples, or maybe they'd had a very definite reason for targeting the village.

Brice didn't want to voice his worries, but he was beginning to think someone within the clinic had double-crossed this ugly gang of bandits. Must have been a pretty big deal for them to come in and kill just about everyone. Had they been angry or searching for something? He'd need an inventory of whatever drugs and equipment might be missing. That is, if he could get someone to venture into the abandoned clinic to find, what, if anything, was left. Selena had indicated that a small crew of villagers might still be trying to keep it open, but from what he could find no one had set foot on the spot since the attack. Dr. Jarrell had confirmed that the first time they'd met, but then none of them had any way of knowing exactly what was going on down there. Maybe he could get someone on his CHAIM team to check into that. So far, all he had to go on were several reports of illegal smuggling and gun trafficking, and Día Belo was located near the main route for all that illegal activity. He needed a solid connection between the clinic and the Night Walkers.

He thought about Diego. Maybe he should start there with his next round of research. Diego Reis had been American born and bred right here in Atlanta, but he'd gone down to Argentina because his family roots were Portuguese and he wanted to make a difference in the tiny border village where his ancestors had lived at one time—according to what Delton had told Brice when they'd talked at length the other night. But maybe Diego had gone down there for more than just sentimental reasons. Brice had certainly seen all kinds of motivations for crime and some people could cover their sins with pretty persuasion and a façade.

Selena didn't like to talk about Diego. Maybe because she had feelings for the man? And now, because he was dead? Or maybe because she was trying to valiantly protect her friend? Was she still grieving him as the man she had loved? Or was she just trying to save his honor? Maybe both?

Brice didn't know which drove him to distraction more, the fact that Selena might not trust him enough to tell him everything, or the bitter realization that she might have been so in love with Diego that she was willing to conceal things to protect him even though the man was dead.

He'd get to the heart of the matter. He always did. But that would mean having to interrogate Selena. And he hated to do that. Might be a necessary thing—as his friend Eli Trudeau would say.

Brice pulled his papers together, remembering one

of his grandmother's sayings. "A man may live after losing his life but not after losing his honor." Maybe Selena wanted to save Diego's honor.

"Quoting poetry to yourself?"

He turned to find Selena standing at the door of the anteroom where he'd been hanging out most of the day while she worked. "No, luv. Just musing out loud. One of my granny's wise old sayings. She was all about honor and doing the right thing."

"Careful," Selena said with a tired smile. "Your Irish is showing."

He had to grin at that. When they'd first met, he'd been so determined to fit in here in America, he'd tried to hide his Irish roots. But arguing with Selena always raised his dander and brought out his brogue. Hard to hide anything from this woman.

So why was she trying so hard to hide something from him?

He took in her daisy-covered green scrubs and her upswept hair. She'd been a bit quiet and distant since they'd kissed the other night, but at least her spunk had returned. "Are you all done then?"

"I am. We had a pretty good day today. No deaths and very few emergencies. The full moon is next week so things will probably heat up and get crazy. But for now, it's Friday and I'm ready to get out of here."

He pushed away from the small, battered desk. "How about that—it is Friday."

"Yes and that means your week is up."

Brice shot out of his chair. "Not so fast, princess."

Her frown was cute but fierce. "You said a week, Brice."

"I said *at least* a week. This is not over, Selena. I think it's only just beginning."

She looked down at the floor. "But I want to go back to my apartment. I want to have my life back."

"I'll take you—just to pick up some things."

"This is silly. Nothing has happened…since the bombing."

He noticed the way she avoided looking directly at him when she said that. Interesting. "That doesn't mean a thing and you know it. A lot could be happening behind the scenes and we just haven't seen it yet."

"What do you mean? Have you heard something?"

There it was again—that trace of evasiveness. He'd seen it in her eyes over and over during the past week. And he had just about reached his limit on evasion. Besides, it wasn't like Selena to be that way. He had to make her talk to him somehow.

"Let's get out of here," he said, grabbing her by the arm before she could protest. "I'm thinking a nice steak and maybe some movies at home."

"But—"

"But, I am not going to let you go out there on your own until I solve this problem. You're comfortable at my house, right?"

"Of course. More than comfortable."

"And everyone there has been kind to you?"

"Yes, extremely patient and kind. I have no complaints."

"Okay, then I'd suggest you stay comfy and cozy at my house. Just through the weekend, all right?"

"But…I have things I want to do this weekend."

"Such as?"

"Dr. Jarrell invited me to his house out on Lake Lanier. He's having a cookout."

Brice's hackles went up. "Really? And why wasn't I told about this?"

"Maybe because he just invited me about two minutes ago as he was heading out the back door."

"Oh. Well, tell him you can't go."

She put her hands on her hips, her eyes defiant. "That would be rude. I've been out there lots of times. It's a big, private compound."

Brice pushed at his nose. He was getting a headache. "Do you have a certain longing to see the lake, luv?"

"It would be nice, yes. It's spring and everything is so pretty out there this time of year. I could use the fresh air."

"Have you noticed the pollen?"

"Yes, but the rain the other day knocked a lot of that down, and besides, pollen is better than being inside all weekend."

Well, she was certainly *knocking down* every roadblock he was setting up for her. "You can see flowers in my garden."

"I'm going to the lake, Brice, and that's final."

He came close, then leaned into her face. "Okay. Then I'm going with you."

She started to complain, then shut her mouth. "If you insist."

"I do."

He would make her talk to him if it took tossing her pretty little self into the lake. And it just might come to that. Didn't she see the danger? Didn't she feel in her gut, as he did in his, that this was far from over? The people who'd destroyed her beloved village were still out there and this silence was driving him crazy, making him antsy. And until he had her safety secured, he'd have to stay by her side whether she liked it or not.

She didn't like this. Selena hated keeping things from Brice, but all week long she'd tried to muster the courage to tell him about the cell phone call. But if she did that, she'd have to tell him everything else and she wasn't ready for that. Not until she had solid evidence back from the toxicology report. Since she hadn't received any more calls and things at Brice's estate seemed normal and quiet, she'd somehow convinced herself it wasn't as bad as she'd imagined. She'd at least found a way to have the pills she'd found at Mr. Cooper's home analyzed, too. She knew people who could do this without involving the law, but what if someone heard about it and questioned her for taking the pills in the first place? How could she explain why she'd lifted Mr. Cooper's nitroglycerin and Digoxin? Too late now. She'd sent the pills to a local lab that was also used to analyzing fake Ecstasy—to protect clueless teenagers at rave parties—but her source had promised to be discreet since the site promised anonymity for all. She prayed for good results on both of the reports. And she also prayed for forgiveness from both God and Brice.

She'd dug this hole so deep, she didn't know how to get out. Maybe she should talk to Dr. Jarrell. He'd certainly understand her need to have the pills analyzed. Both the pills she'd taken from Mr. Cooper's house and the pills she'd found on the clinic floor that horrible day—some of which she still carried in her tote. If she confided in him instead of Brice, this whole thing could be cleared up without bringing CHAIM down on the clinic in Día Belo. She couldn't bear permanently shutting down either of the clinics. She'd worked so hard to keep both clinics up and running and her parents had given a lot of funding to her causes. But CHAIM wouldn't continue backing either if something illegal was taking place. Best to get this cleared up very quietly and hope that in the meantime Brice would find the real culprits. Of course, if she did find something suspicious in the toxicology reports, then, by law she'd have to report her findings immediately.

Selena lowered her head and shut her eyes, praying for some relief. The stress of the last few weeks was beginning to take its toll on her.

A knock at her bedroom door jolted her back. "Are you ready?"

Brice. He was determined to go with her to Dr. Jarrell's lake house today. Selena didn't mind him going but his presence wouldn't make for a relaxing afternoon. Every time she looked at him she became torn between her secrets and her longings. How could she find some private time with Dr. Jarrell to talk to him about her concerns? And how was she supposed to put that kiss out of her head when Brice was always around, always giving her that wry smile of his?

"Are you going to open the door, *cara?*"

She hurried across the room. "Sorry. Just woolgathering."

Brice leaned against the jamb, his eyes moving over her face in a keen search that left her breathless. "Are you sure you're up to this?"

"I'm very up for this. I told you, I need some fresh air and as much as I love your home, I need to get out of here for just a few hours. We're not going to argue about this all the way to the lake, are we?"

"Oh, no. If the lady wants to go to the lake, then that's where we'll go. But we do need to establish a few ground rules."

"No rules today, Brice. Please?"

He didn't move out of the doorway as she tried to pass. "We have to have rules, Selena. For your protection."

Holding her beach bag close, she shook her head. "Oh, all right. If that's the only way you'll let me leave this house, then I guess I can listen."

He moved out of the way, then followed her across the landing to the stairs. "First, you stay within my sight at all times, understand?"

"As if you'd let me out of your sight," she countered, her tennis shoes hitting the winding stairs.

"That is correct. I will be watching you at all times."

"Got it. Brice is watching."

"Don't be coy now. And second, don't talk to anyone you don't know. Not even to say hello."

"That won't make for very much conversation. Dr. Jarrell usually has a lot of people at these get-togethers."

"And that brings me to three. We won't be staying until dark. It's just too risky."

She stopped at the bottom of the stairs. "But that's the best part. He has lights all along the deck out to the lake and sometimes people take the boats out to watch the sunset."

"We'll catch the sunset on the way back into the city."

They reached the side door past the kitchen. Adele sat at the long butcher block table reading the *Atlanta Journal-Constitution* while she sipped her tea. "Are you off?"

"We're about to leave," Brice replied. "We might be late getting back. Don't make any dinner for us."

"I might not be here either," Adele replied with a smile. "Beatrice and I are going to see a play at the Alliance—the matinee—and maybe an early dinner at The Varsity."

Surprised, Selena whirled around. "You're going out this afternoon with my mother? And to The Varsity? Chili dogs and fries? That's certainly a switch from her usual tearoom luncheons."

Adele lifted her chin, her eyes twinkling. "Not to mention onion rings and pie. And yes, we thought we'd enjoy a bit of Georgia Tech nostalgia. I hope that's not a concern."

"No, not at all. I just didn't know you two were that close," Selena replied.

Adele chuckled. "Worrying about our children tends to do that to mothers. We have to stick together and eating junk food at a local landmark seems to help." She lifted her shoulders in a feminine shrug. "We had a nice long talk after dinner the other night. I think we bonded."

Brice came back into the long, sunny kitchen to give his mother a kiss on the cheek. "Don't worry, Mum, bond all you want. You know I'm going to make things right."

"You always do," Adele replied, her blue eyes

moving from Brice to Selena. "Just be careful. This is a very dangerous thing."

"I'm always careful."

Selena watched Brice's mother as he stepped back. Her presence here had put a strain on all of them, in spite of their warm hospitality and kind concern. "I'm sorry, Mrs. Whelan," she said. "I've brought this on you."

Adele got up to put her tea cup in the sink. "Don't be ridiculous, darling. Since the day my son joined CHAIM, I've worried. But God prefers prayers to tears. So I pray."

"And she keeps smiling," Brice said, grinning. "I love you, Mum."

Adele patted his face. "Go on, now. Have fun."

Selena saw the love between mother and son. She was blessed to have that kind of love in her family, too. And she certainly knew the constant worry her mother had tried to hide. CHAIM was a good, strong organization in spite of the recent illegal activity one of its most powerful members had brought into the organization. But Eli Trudeau, along with Brice and former CHAIM agent Devon Malone, had brought all of that to a halt. Now, Brice was focused on protecting her.

Maybe she should be a bit more gracious. Closing her eyes for a brief prayer, she asked God to help her and to give her the strength to be honest with Brice.

He tugged her out toward the long, multidoored garage, his expression focused now that they were away from his mother. "Let's take the Jag today. We'll put the top down if I see we're all clear."

Selena smiled at that. "I'd forgotten what a car enthusiast you are. I guess sheep farming is really paying off these days."

"Sheep farming doesn't make my money, luv," he said, hitting the remote to the garage. "You know that most of my inheritance came from my mother's side of the family."

She shook her head. "I remember you hinting at that, but it's impolite to ask such things, so no, I didn't know for sure." And even though he'd been an open book with her on most things, he'd never talked much about his deceased Irish father or their ancestral home, maybe because it was now a stronghold for CHAIM. "I just assumed…I mean, you own a castle."

"Aye, that I do and yes, it came down from my father's side of the family but the castle is funded heavily by CHAIM, since it's considered an official CHAIM site. We worked out a deal on that long ago. I work for CHAIM and CHAIM maintains my ancestral home in return for the use of it for meetings and retreats and such. I get to keep the sheep farm and our mills running and they do bring in a bit of a profit, but it's never easy."

He took her things and tossed them in the boot of the vintage black Jaguar sports car, then helped her into the aged gray leather seat. "My mother comes from old southern money. She's a bona fide blue-blooded Atlanta aristocrat with a lineage that dates back well before the Civil War. Not as many centuries as my father's clan, but aristocratic nonetheless."

"That's considered royalty here," Selena said. "My mother used to tell me about your parents' lineage but we didn't want to gossip so we just left it at that. Why haven't you ever told me more about this?"

"Didn't think it was necessary. I thought everyone in Atlanta knew about the beautiful American heiress who went to Ireland on a spring trip and fell in love with the last remaining Whelan of the Castle Whelan. It's a highly romantic tale that produced a male boy to carry on the name."

"And yet, you don't mention that and you don't brag. You always said they'd met one spring and that was that. Love at first sight."

"Would it have mattered if I'd told you any differently?"

"No, of course not. I didn't care where you were from or how much money you had. I just knew you were different and refreshing…and a good friend."

"I'm glad. I wanted to keep a low profile."

Selena understood then. Brice had a keen sense of heritage. His Irish background meant a lot to him, considering his father had died when he was still in high school. "You didn't want to come to America, did you?"

"Nope. But mum was lonely in Ireland after my father passed. It's hard living in a castle when the man you loved died from a massive heart attack right there riding his stallion in the meadow beyond the cliffs."

"I'm so sorry," Selena said. Then she smiled over at him as the wind picked up her ponytail and fanned it out around her face. "But…I'm glad you came to Atlanta. I don't know what I would have done in college without you. You always knew so much about European history and literature."

"Aye, well, I kind of lived through a bit of it, now didn't I?"

"I suppose you did. Now I'm even more impressed."

"So now that you know I come from a long line of southern royalty—at least by half—does that make your cold heart open up to me just a bit more?"

She laughed out loud. "My heart has always been open to you, Brice."

"Really now?"

His smile caused her to take in a breath. The way his eyes slid over her, all amber and shining like a lion watching its prey, made her get little goose bumps on her arms in spite of the warm day. "Yes," she admitted. "You have my heart, because I know you'll keep it safe."

"I will, indeed." He shifted gears as they reached a main thoroughfare and headed out into the Saturday morning traffic, then he slanted his gaze back toward her. "That is, if you'll just let me."

The look he gave her told Selena that he *knew.* He knew she was hiding something from him. But how could she explain? How could she be sure about anything?

She glanced back over at him, taking in the way the morning sun sparkled through his burnished shaggy hair. He was a handsome man, his face hard and angled and edged with shadows and light and scars. Brice was also an honest, devout man, his heart softened by the light of Christ and the love of a strong family—and a few scars there, too.

Would he ever forgive her for what she considered her necessary omissions? Selena hoped so. And she prayed she'd find the courage to tell him everything that burdened her heart. Because if she couldn't talk to her best friend, then who could she talk to?

EIGHT

Brice had an itchy feeling. Call it instinct, call it crazy, but something about Dr. Jarrell's expansive lake house gave him a case of the willies. Maybe it was the thick foliage of lush green oaks and tall pines, or the hilly terrain nestled in the foothills of the Appalachian Mountains. Couple that with too many happy, laughing people and, well, it made his skin crawl. He tried to relax as he stood on the wide wooden deck and gazed out over the sloping yard toward what Selena had called a party dock down on the water. But he didn't like this, not one bit. He'd never been one for crowds anyway. And this fun-loving crowd seemed intent on racing boats and Jet Skis and pushing people in the water—whether they wanted to get wet or not.

"Could you at least smile?" Selena asked, handing him a cup of soda. "The dogwoods and wisterias are blooming, the azaleas are divine and the breeze off the lake is wonderful. Don't you love this place?"

"Aye, love it." He took a long swig of the bubbly drink to hide his disapproval. "I didn't realize the clinic pays enough for such a lavish second home."

Frowning, she shook her head. "You know we don't get paid very much. Dr. Jarrell is also on staff at one of the big hospitals and his wife is a highly regarded professor. And besides, he's really good with investing his money. Does that explain things to you?"

Seeing the spark of irritation in her eyes, he nodded. "Perfectly."

But it almost seemed too perfect to Brice. And he had to wonder if maybe he shouldn't be checking into the good doctor's background, too.

Selena, however, seemed to take it all in stride. Dr. Jarrell was a friend of her father's and a trusted physician who mingled in high-class circles and gave a lot of time and money to several local charities. But a background check on the man couldn't hurt, could it?

Or maybe Brice was just being overly protective and suspicious of everyone around him. He was trained to be that way, of course, but that didn't mean he had to accuse people without reason. Hoping to salvage the day, he turned to Selena. "Why don't we walk down to the boat dock and join in the fun?"

"Are you sure?" she asked, her eyes blazing like a fire's tip. "We wouldn't want to be sociable, now would we?"

"I'm sure." He took her by the elbow. "It would be rude to stand up here and stare while everyone else is having such a rollicking good time."

She lifted her black sunshades to stare over at him. "Are you being sincere or sarcastic?"

"Completely sincere," he replied, but not for the reason she thought. He wanted to check out the crowd. "Let's get down there."

They were heading down the wide, planked steps when the doctor and his wife came strolling up the path. "Selena, there you are," Dr. Jarrell said, smiling. "I'm so glad you made it." He gave Brice a pasty smile. "And I see you brought your sidekick."

Selena sent Brice a warning glance. "I hope you don't mind. I hate attending parties by myself and, well, Brice insisted on bringing me."

"Of course we don't mind, darling." Liz Jarrell, a pretty green-eyed blonde wearing a cap-sleeved blue sweater and crisp white capris, patted Selena on the arm. "Considering what you've been through, it's no wonder you're afraid to venture out alone."

"I'm fine," Selena assured her, her eyes shadowed with doubt. "Just a precaution."

"And a very wise one," Dr. Jarrell said. "Brice is a capable companion. We hardly even noticed him hanging around the clinic this week but we all felt immensely better having him there."

Brice tried to keep his tight smile in place, thinking how very much he felt like a gnat right now—hanging around, buzzing around, being a wee little nuisance.

"How long will this go on?" Liz asked, her expression laced with just enough concern to keep her Botox injections intact.

Brice finally spoke. "As long as it takes."

Selena's chuckle was forced. "Brice takes his duties very seriously, but hopefully today we can forget about this for a while and just relax."

"That sounds like a splendid plan," Dr. Jarrell said. "Liz, take this young lady down to the party. Brice, would you mind helping me bring down the steaks?"

"Of course not," Brice said, his gaze moving from Selena to the doctor. "But Selena—"

"I'll be fine," Selena said, reading his mind. "You can see the dock from the house."

Dr. Jarrell nodded. "I have the steaks right inside but I need a helping hand to get them down to the grill."

Short of being rude, Brice had no choice but to go inside the massive kitchen with the doctor. At least this side of the house was mostly all windows so he did have a clear view of the dock and the water.

"Here you go," Dr. Jarrell said, handing Brice a big baking pan heavy with steaks and chicken. "Hope you're hungry. I grill a mean, lean steak and I cook chicken just right—for the ladies. They prefer it, I think."

Brice laughed. "You've covered all the bases."

"I try," Dr. Jarrell said, his tone blunt and firm, his smile plastered across his face like the grill of a muscle car. "And I believe you do the same, right?"

"Right," Brice said, playing along with this male bonding gig.

Dr. Jarrell lifted a hip toward the open French door, indicating that Brice should follow him outside. "You know, we're all very fond of Selena. I've known her since she was born because I helped deliver her. I'd never want anything to happen to her."

"Neither would I, sir."

"I'm glad we have an understanding then."

Puzzled at that comment and the doctor's tone, Brice stopped on the flagstone path. "Is there something more you'd like to say?"

Dr. Jarrell held his tray close. "No, no. I just wanted

you to know we're taking this threat seriously. I sent Selena and Diego down to Argentina, so I feel responsible for this tragedy. And I won't tolerate anyone trying to harm Selena now that she's home. We might not be able to keep the Día Belo clinic up and running, but we will stop any threats here at home, I can assure you."

Brice wanted to be assured and he wanted to feel *reassured*. But somehow, he didn't. "I appreciate that. Selena's safety is my main concern."

"And mine, too." The doctor started back down the path. "Just let me know if I can help you in any way. If you have any questions about our operations both here and down there, just come to me, okay?"

Brice understood. The doctor wanted to be in on all the details of the CHAIM investigation. Even though he didn't know Brice worked for the secretive organization, he did know Brice had been hired as a bodyguard by Selena's father. He wanted to be in the loop since his clinic was in jeopardy and since CHAIM had been a silent, anonymous backer through Selena's efforts and her father's advisement to their church board. But confiding in the doctor would mean having to divulge sensitive information, something Brice couldn't do, regardless of this nice little man-to-man chat.

Glancing down at where Selena stood laughing with her coworker Meg and some others, Brice said, "I'll let you know if I need anything, sir. Thanks."

Dr. Jarrell sent him one final appraising look, then turned on the charm for the large group mingling down by the water. "Let's get these steaks cooking, shall we?"

Brice heard a loud chorus of agreement while he wondered just what else the good doctor had cooking.

* * *

Selena enjoyed the warmth of the sun on her cheeks. It was nice to forget all her worries and laugh with the many volunteers and friends of the clinic. Dr. Jarrell had a wide circle of supporters, some of them very high up in local politics and social circles. He'd always been devoted to making the clinic work, and somehow, he always managed to secure more funding almost exactly when they needed it. Thankful that God had granted them this opportunity to make a difference in the inner city, she said a quick prayer of gratitude. Then Dr. Jarrell himself came strolling up.

"How are you, really?" he asked, glancing around to make sure no one was listening.

Selena looked around, too. Brice was getting something to drink and bringing back dessert. Maybe now would be a good time to ask Dr. Jarrell a few questions since they rarely had any time at the clinic. "I'm okay. I'm still in shock but I'm doing better. Dr. Jarrell, did you know the gang down in Día Belo took most of the drugs we had stocked in our on-site pharmacy?"

He nodded, then lowered his voice. "Yes, I did. I think that's why they attacked us. Probably smuggled the medication on the black market to make a pretty penny. Disgusting, but a reality."

"But why now?" Selena asked. "They never bothered us before."

"I can't answer that, Selena." He gave her a puzzled stare. "Do you remember something? Anything that might explain what happened?"

Selena shook her head, praying she'd have enough time before Brice came back to tell him her fears. "I don't remember anything that stands out, but I'm beginning to wonder if maybe someone at the clinic made this group angry. What if one of the villagers or one of our workers made a deal with the Night Walkers and then reneged on it? That would explain the brutal attack."

"It would indeed," the doctor said, his expression grim. "But we'll probably never find out the whole truth." He leaned closer. "Are you sure you don't remember anything more about this?"

She hesitated, then looked up at him. "I'm sorry, no. I've got another theory, though. But I can't be sure. A few days before the attack we had a villager get very sick after taking some cholesterol medicine. You remember the new one we ordered for both the pharmacy here and the one at the clinic?"

He nodded, then cleared his throat. "Yes— supposed to be the latest and best, based on extensive research. So you think someone got ill after taking that medicine?"

"I don't know if it was the medicine or not and that's what concerns me. She came in right before the attack so I never got a chance to investigate." But Selena had taken the returned pills, the pills she'd found spilled on the floor. She didn't tell the doctor that, though. Instead, she said, "The woman believed the medicine had made her sick. What if the pills were…tainted?"

Dr. Jarrell took her by the elbow and led her away from the others. "Tainted in what way?"

Selena couldn't find a good way to say it, so she just blurted it out. "What if the medicine was substandard or maybe even fake? We both know that's a growing problem internationally."

Dr. Jarrell's frown turned ruddy. "That can't be. I personally oversee every drug we order for both sites. Impossible. The patient survived, right?"

"Yes, but—"

"You're imagining things, Selena. You're just overworked and still a bit distraught. I know you want to get to the bottom of this, but don't go creating more anxiety for yourself. Do I need to prescribe you a sedative?"

Offended at his condescending tone, Selena shook her head. "No, no. I'm fine. I just thought you should know."

"Well, that's silly. Just put that theory out of your head, okay. Concentrate on taking care of our patients here for now." He looked at his watch, then said, "I have to make a call. Just checking on a patient." With that, he stomped up toward the house.

"All right." She watched as he hurried off, not sure if he was relieved or aggravated by their conversation. But apparently, he didn't believe anything illegal could be going on in their clinics or their pharmacies. Selena wasn't so sure. And she intended to dig deeper to find out where they ordered their drugs and how. But she'd have to be very careful and very discreet. She didn't want both Brice and Dr. Jarrell coming down on her for snooping around on her own.

Turning to search for Brice, she saw him heading back toward her. Selena sat down on a chair and closed her eyes, the warmth of the sun covering the chill of dread that seemed to overtake her. She had to put this out of her mind for now or Brice would notice something was bothering her.

* * *

"Your nose is getting red."

An hour later, Selena opened her eyes to find Brice smiling at her. Forcing a cheery attitude, she said, "I put on sunscreen."

He took her plate of leftover dessert. She'd only nibbled at the pound cake and peaches. "Just checking," he said, his expression blank now.

Did the man think she didn't have a brain? Of course, she'd lathered on the sunscreen. She didn't want to burn but she did want to enjoy getting a light tan, at least. Brice's fidgeting and fussing was beginning to make her more nervous instead of more relaxed. And her talk with Dr. Jarrell hadn't helped matters. Was it her imagination or had the doctor been avoiding her for the last hour or so?

To change her mood, she motioned toward the sleek speedboat anchored at the dock. "Want to take a spin?"

Brice's eyes lit up. "On that go-fast thing, who wouldn't?"

"Then let's go. Dr. Jarrell won't mind." And she could use the distraction.

"Whoa." His hand held her arm. "Not so fast, princess."

Selena saw the deep frown burrowing his brow. "What's wrong?"

"I'm just not so sure you should be out on the water. Puts you in a vulnerable position—too open. It's risky."

Selena's anger surfaced right along with a swimmer coming up for air by the big floating inner tube out past the dock. Why did all the men in her life think she couldn't do anything for herself? "Brice, honestly, don't you think you're being just a bit overly cautious? I don't think anyone would dare follow me out here. There are too many people around."

"That won't matter to someone with a high-powered rifle, luv. It's too dangerous. I'd rather you stick close to the house."

Defiant and frustrated, she shook her head. "And I'd rather take a ride on the boat before we have to leave."

"It's getting late, Selena. The sun's going down."

"Yes, and I'd love to watch it setting behind the trees from that boat out on the lake."

"I don't think—"

"I don't care what you think, Brice. Just let me have some fun and then I'll go back to the city with you, no complaints."

She acknowledged that she was taking out her frustrations on him but if she stopped to think about things, she'd stalk off on her own. Better to try and pretend for now. And ignore the red flags going up inside her mind.

He glanced out at the water, then back at her, his eyes dark and foreboding. "Fine, but I'm going with you—just the two of us."

"I can handle that," she replied, her heart thumping like the waves hitting the dock. Being alone with him on the water with the sun going down wouldn't exactly relax her but at least she'd won part of this battle. "Let's go."

Together, they walked along the hilly shore toward the waiting boat. Selena spotted Dr. Jarrell sitting on the stone patio carved into the hills high above the dock. "Hi. Mind if Brice and I go out on the speedboat?"

"Of course not," Dr. Jarrell said, excusing himself from the group clustered on the comfortable chairs around the massive rock outdoor fireplace. Glancing toward the house, he said, "Actually, I was planning on taking you out with Liz but I don't mind Brice being the captain instead." He stared over at Brice. "I assume you know how to drive one of those things."

"I think I can manage," Brice replied with a quiet smile.

He'd been trained to drive anything with an engine, but the doctor didn't need to know that, Selena thought, confident that she would indeed be safe with Brice. Feeling a bit contrite for her earlier outburst, she gave him a reassuring smile. "Thanks."

"Let me just go down and clear out a few things, then she's all yours," Dr. Jarrell said, his hands on his hips. "I'll be back in a few minutes, Liz. If you get cold, just start the fire. I've got the logs all ready."

His wife waved him away, then turned back to her friends. "Men and their toys."

Selena and Brice followed the doctor out onto the dock. Brice helped her onto the boat behind the doctor, then hopped in.

Dr. Jarrell glanced around again. "Oh, we're missing a life jacket. Brice, would you mind going back up to the storage shed to get one? We have several in there but there's only one on here. I wouldn't want the game warden to give us a ticket."

Brice glanced toward Selena with a mixture of agitation and concern. "We don't have to go out if it's too much trouble."

"Not at all," Dr. Jarrell said. "I just need that life jacket. Now hurry or you'll miss the sunset."

"I can go get it," Selena offered, sensing Brice was about to abort the whole boat ride over this one sticking point.

"No," he said, getting back out of the boat. "I'll get the life jacket and I'll be right back. Sit tight."

Selena nodded, understanding that he was not pleased with this request. Dr. Jarrell had a habit of bossing people around and now it seemed he was testing Brice to see how strong his mettle was. He'd soon find out, she reasoned, wondering if the doctor was just concerned about her and their earlier discussion and taking it out on Brice.

"He's sure highly wired, isn't he?" Dr. Jarrell said with a chuckle.

He seemed as skittish as a tomcat himself. Why had she worried him with her irrational imaginings?

To cover her humiliation, she said, "Yes. Brice has always been intense, but he means well."

"Listen, you haven't mentioned any of your concerns to him, have you?"

Selena took a quick look up toward the house. "No. You're the only one I've talked to about that. And I'm sorry I even brought it up. I guess I'm just a bit paranoid. And so is Brice. But…that bomb was pretty scary."

"I can understand. And I admire Brice's dedication. He's very protective of you but I have a feeling it's not all about the danger you're in. I think the man has feelings for you."

Was the attraction between them that obvious? Selena gave him a dismissive shrug. "We're just close. It's been that way since college."

Dr. Jarrell pivoted toward the boat shed. "It's taking him a long time. Maybe I'd better go check."

He stepped back onto the dock before Selena could

protest. She sat on the rocking boat, dusk gathering around her, and watched as everyone else up above her on the hillside laughed and mingled. Dr. Jarrell stopped for a brief time to talk to another man who'd just come down from the house. The man looked toward where Selena sat, a soft smile centered on his face. Wondering where Brice had gone and why it was taking him so long, she started to get out of the boat.

Then she heard footsteps on the dock and looked up to find that same man approaching her. "Hi," he said, grinning. "I've been dying to take this sweet baby out on the open water."

With that, he jumped in the boat and pushed past Selena to get to the steering wheel. "Hold on, okay? I like to travel really fast."

"Who are you?" Selena asked, trying to stand.

The man, handsome and mysterious—too mysterious in spite of his white teeth and winning good looks— didn't respond. Instead, he cranked the boat and throttled it into a fast swirl of water and wind, causing Selena to fall back against the padded cushion of her seat. Grabbing on, she took in a gulp of startled breath as a cool spray of damp mist hit her with each bounce of the fast-moving boat.

"Selena? Selena!"

Panicked now and not sure how to get out of this situation, she glanced helplessly toward the shore and saw Brice running along the dock, calling after her, the extra life jacket clutched to his chest.

While both he and the shore grew farther and farther away.

NINE

Brice dropped the forgotten life jacket, his heart roaring to life as blood rushed through his temples, pounding against his system like a crashing wave. He had to do something. Turning, he saw Dr. Jarrell standing on the dock by the shore. Brice didn't stop to think; he just rushed toward the smiling doctor and grabbed him by his yellow polo shirt. "Who was that man?"

Dr. Jarrell looked shocked, then pushed at Brice's arms. "Relax, he's an intern at the hospital. He thinks Selena is pretty and wanted some alone time with her."

"You let her go out there with someone else, knowing what she's been through?"

The doctor frowned, then shrugged. "I trust Greg. He's harmless. And besides, you were smothering her. The girl needed a break."

Brice shook his head, anger coursing through his pores. "She looked terrified." Then he put a finger on the doctor's chest. "If something happens to her—"

"She's fine," Dr. Jarrell said, pushing Brice's hand away. "Young man, you need to lighten up."

Brice wanted to toss the obstinate man into the water, but he had to get out there and find Selena. Looking around at the now silent crowd, he focused on a couple sitting on a Jet Ski at the water's edge. Hopping off the dock, Brice ran toward them. "Get off," he shouted. "I need to borrow this."

He didn't wait for them to move, but the young girl looked frightened so she quickly climbed away, calling her companion as she ran from Brice's fierce shouting.

The young fellow stood his ground, guarding the Jet Ski. "Hey, man—"

"I need this now!" Brice said, easily lifting the scrawny teen off the Jet Ski. Before the boy could protest, Brice had it shoved into deeper water and cranked. Then he took off toward the direction of the boat, praying he'd find Selena safe and sound.

"So you work at the clinic, huh?"

Selena nodded at the tan, muscular man, trying to decide how to get herself out of this mess. She hated to admit it, but Brice had been right. She should have been more aware and careful. Wouldn't he enjoy holding that over her head?

She wanted Brice to come and find her, right now, but she also knew how to take care of herself. Especially with overly zealous men. It was obvious that Greg—or Gregory Gordon III, as he'd introduced himself after pulling the boat up inside this hidden cove—had been drinking too much. Brice didn't drink; Selena knew this. Neither one of them did. She never realized how much she appreciated that quality about him until now. As darkness fell and the bright coral-colored sun sank off to the west, Selena felt a chill descending over her. She wasn't wearing her hoodie and her arms were cold. And she'd missed sharing the incredible sunset with Brice. That made her even madder.

So cold and so dumb. Why hadn't she been more careful?

She looked at the now-black water, then glanced back at the man grinning over at her. "This is nice, but we need to get back."

"Ah, now, we were just getting to know each other," Greg said, stumbling toward her. "It's private and quiet here. Pleasant, don't you think?"

"Not really," Selena replied, tired and frustrated and willing to take matters into her own hands. "I don't know you and I'd like to go back to the party now. I mean it."

Greg looked perplexed. "But Dr. Jarrell—"

"Dr. Jarrell will want his boat back and my friend will be worried about me." And you do not want to provoke Brice, buddy.

Greg sank down beside her, tugging her close. She could smell the alcohol on his breath. "Not so fast, sunshine. I thought you'd be the life of the party and now…you're really bringing me down."

Selena had been trained in self-defense—anyone related to a CHAIM agent was always trained to take care of themselves. But right now she felt frozen, not so much in fear, but frozen in her own defiance and stubbornness. If she'd listened to Brice, she wouldn't be in this mess now.

I've learned my lesson, Lord. I need his help and I need You. After coming home, she'd somehow managed to forget that she needed God in her life at all times. She'd been so busy blaming Brice for cramping her style and so worried about what she'd find in the toxicology reports she'd secretly requested, she'd overlooked what a blessing Brice was in her life and that she'd appealed to her Lord to help her on that horrible day. He'd sent her a real hero. He'd sent her Brice. She'd never take that for granted again.

But right now, she had to protect herself from this drunken idiot. So she stood up, her gaze moving over the boat until it settled on an oar lying in the damp bottom near the cushioned storage bench. Moving toward the front of the boat, she said, "I'll drive us home."

"I'm not ready to go home," Greg said, his words slurred, his voice petulant. "Besides, we really need to talk about some things." He pushed at her, his goofy grin turning into a sinister frown. "Quit ruining all my fun. Sit down and shut up!"

Selena stood back up, bracing herself against one of the seats to quell the nausea rising up inside her stomach. "I don't want to sit down and I'm not staying here with you!"

With that, she pushed past him and grabbed the paddle. Then she turned toward him, intent on whacking him over the head. But in spite of being tipsy, Greg still had enough of his faculties to lunge toward her. And when he did, he pushed her right toward the sloping edge of the sleek boat. Selena screamed and tried to balance herself but the weight of the paddle in one hand and Greg pushing at her other arm proved too much. The paddle fell and skidded across the bottom of the boat while she lost her balance.

Selena screamed again, her body hitting against the side of the boat just as Greg lunged for her again. She was going overboard and there was nothing she could do but let go and fall into the cold, dark water.

Brice had searched all over this part of the lake. Had the man taken Selena to another location? Trying to keep his cool, he thought back over the moment he'd seen the boat leaving the dock. He was sure it had come in this direction, but with the fading light and the shadows from the trees, it was hard to see anything. Even if he had to call in a search team, he wasn't leaving here without Selena.

Then he heard a scream.

Throttling the Jet Ski, he pushed it toward a small island near the shore, then circled the island in a rush of water and waves.

The boat was moored underneath ancient oaks shrouded in Spanish moss. As Brice brought the Jet Ski skidding to a halt in the shallow water, he looked up and saw Selena struggling with the man.

And then he watched in horror as she stumbled against the side of the boat and fell headfirst into the water.

Going into action, Brice jumped off the Jet Ski and swam toward the boat. The water was freezing cold now that the sun had gone down. If she'd been knocked out, she wouldn't last long down there.

Spotting the man slumped over in the boat seat, Brice vowed to deal with him later. Right now, he had to get to Selena. He dove under the water near where Selena had fallen in, but this near the shore, the water was dark and murky with weeds and shrubs. Tall grasses tore at his feet and arms, but he kept pushing. Then he surfaced, spitting water as he looked around.

"Selena?"

He heard a moan from a clump of gnarled tree stumps near the shore. Swimming, then running, he pushed through the mud. "Selena?"

She lay half in, half out of the dark, lapping water. "Brice?"

"I'm here. Right here." He saw her there in the light from the rising moon, clinging to the broken, aged stumps. "Are you all right?"

"Cold," she said through a shudder. "Cold. I think I hit my head."

Brice reached out to her, pulling her into his arms. "It's all right." He held her tight, thinking how small she felt, his fingers moving over her face and head. He felt a rising bump near her right temple.

"Ouch!" She was shivering, probably more from fright and shock than the actual cold.

"C'mon," he said, taking her up into his arms. "Let's get you somewhere warm and dry so we can check that wound better."

She didn't argue with him. But she did mumble something against his chest as he waded through the shallow water. "What is it, luv?"

"I'm sorry," she said, her voice low and whispery. "I'm so stupid."

In spite of aging ten years in the past ten minutes, he had to agree with that and it made him smile, only because he had her in his arms and he didn't want to let her go. "I'll forgive you this time. But don't let it happen again."

Then he gently lifted her into the boat, jumped in behind her and grabbed the now passed out Gregory. Pulling the man up and shaking him, Brice shouted, "Hey, wake up. You don't want to miss the rest of the party, do you?"

Gregory roused, grinning. "No, man. Sure don't. I'm supposed to—"

"Good then," Brice said, interrupting his mutterings. Then he raised his fist in the air. "Because I really want you to remember this."

He wanted to slam his fist into the man's jaw, but before he could, Gregory passed out and went limp in his arms. Throwing him down on the cushioned seat, Brice turned back to Selena, grabbing a beach blanket off one of the benches to wrap around her. After checking her over for any more bruises or welts, he said, "Hold on and try to stay awake, okay? Don't pass out on me. I have to tie up the Jet Ski."

Selena waved a hand in the air. "I'm fine, really. Just a bruise or two. Go."

After securing the Jet Ski to the back of the boat, he came back to Selena. "Do you want to lie down?"

She sent a shuddering look toward where Gregory lay on the bench seat across from her. "Not with him. I'm coming up by you."

Brice didn't argue with that. He pulled her close and held her on his lap, then started the boat and headed back to the doctor's house. And while he thanked God for helping him to find her, he also thought long and hard about what he might say to the good doctor once he had Selena back on solid ground. And right now, the thoughts running through his head weren't very Christian at all.

* * *

In the end, he almost lost his chance to confront Dr. Jarrell. After they reached the dock, Selena insisted they leave, immediately. Whether from fatigue or embarrassment, Brice couldn't say, but she asked him to respect her wishes.

"Brice, don't make this any worse than it already is. Let's just say our goodbyes and go home. I can't take any more tonight."

"I couldn't agree more," he said. He'd have a talk with the doctor later, however. That was not negotiable. But right now, he just wanted Selena out of here and safe again.

So once they were out of the boat and everyone had calmed down, the doctor and his wife walked them up to the house to tell them goodbye.

"I'm so sorry, Selena," Liz Jarrell said, giving Selena a quick hug. "I had no idea Greg was so drunk. I would have never allowed him to get on that boat with you if I'd noticed." She sent her husband an accusing glance.

Dr. Jarrell had the good grace to look embarrassed. "The same goes for me. Gregory has been after me for weeks now to introduce the two of you and, well, I'm afraid the boy got ahead of himself tonight. I do apologize for allowing him to kidnap you like that. I didn't mean to frighten you." He held her hands in his. "You know you mean the world to me. When Greg sobers up, I intend to give the boy a thorough talking-to. You can count on that."

Brice shot the doctor a challenging look, deciding now *was* a good time to confront him. "I'm counting on it. And…if you can't do the job, I'll be glad to explain things to Greg myself."

"What are you implying?" Dr. Jarrell asked, his eyes slashing fire.

"I'm not implying anything," Brice countered. "I'm telling you—again—you know the danger we're facing. I explained this to you and your entire staff. Selena is a target and by letting that idiot take her out on that lake, you put her at risk. See that it doesn't happen again. Keep that man away from Selena—even when he's stone-cold sober."

"Or?"

Brice wondered if the egotistical doctor was hard of hearing. "Or? Don't you understand? This isn't about you and me or an intern with a crush. This is about protecting Selena. There is no room for argument here."

"Always the overprotective one, aren't you?" Dr. Jarrell said, his tone demeaning. "I told you I'm sorry."

Not good enough, but Brice didn't push it for now. He and the doctor both settled for a good, old-fashioned stare-off, both scowling.

"Henry, let's get back to our guests," Liz suggested, her hand on her husband's arm. "Brice is just concerned. We all are." She looked at Selena again. "And I am truly sorry your visit had to end on such a bad note."

"I'm all right," Selena said, grasping Brice's hands. "No harm done. It did rattle me a little bit but that's because things have been so crazy lately, I'm afraid I'm a little paranoid."

"No surprise, considering how antsy your friend here is," the doctor said. But he did turn to Brice, his eyebrows lifted, his frown relaxing. "But I'm glad he's watching after you, even if he did scare everyone at the party with his James Bond rescue tactics."

Before Brice could comment, Selena spoke up. "He's pretty amazing, isn't he?" She shot a weak grin at Brice, but the plea in her gaze told him she didn't want him to make another scene. "Now, I had a lovely time and I'm ready to go…back to Brice's house and take a long, hot shower and go to bed."

"Good idea," Dr. Jarrell said, touching a finger to the bump on her head. He'd examined her earlier and Brice had noticed he did seem truly concerned that she was all right. "No signs of a concussion, but you might have a powerful headache. Take the necessary pain pills tonight."

"Yes, sir."

Brice put the top up on the Jag to ward off the evening chill. Once they were on the road back toward the city, he looked over at Selena. "How are you feeling?"

She shook her head. "Foolish."

"I was referring to your headache."

"I've got a dull ache. I'll be fine."

He should take this time to lecture her, but he couldn't bring himself to do it. "I'm sorry, Selena," he said instead.

She tilted her head. "For what?"

"For pushing you. I should have backed off and let you enjoy the party."

She glanced straight ahead. "I did enjoy it. I actually enjoyed being there with you. And I hate we didn't get our boat ride."

He took her hand in his, then kissed her knuckles. "I have a boat myself. We'll find a way to watch the sunset together from the water, I promise."

She smiled over at him. "I'll hold you to that."

Brice wanted to tell her that he thought the boat ride she'd been forced to take tonight was no accident. Sure, Gregory Gordon had been drinking, but Dr. Jarrell had allowed him to take Selena out in the water anyway. And for that reason alone, Brice still didn't trust the good doctor. Why would he put Selena in such danger?

That was the question Brice needed to have answered. But he didn't think the doctor would give him the answers he wanted. So he'd just have to find them on his own.

He parked the car just outside the garage, then walked with Selena up to the house, intent on getting her settled and then doing some more investigating. But when he entered the foyer, his mother came rushing out of the den.

"Brice, I'm so glad you're home. I've been so worried."

"What is it?"

"Roderick," Adele said, wringing her hands. "He's been waiting in your office all night. The boy is upset and he insists he has to talk to you and only you but he didn't want me to call you. He said this couldn't go out on the phone lines. He thinks our security system might have been compromised. Something about a breach that caused a shutdown. And he thinks it's his fault."

TEN

"Roderick, slow down and start from the beginning."

Brice pinched his nose with his thumb and forefinger, thinking he might need one of those pain pills Selena had taken. His head was booming.

Roderick, tall and lanky with an Adam's apple that bobbed like a cork each time he took a breath, sank down on a stool at the kitchen counter, putting his head in his hands. "I told you—something fishy is going on with our security system here at the house. I was walking the perimeter of the property earlier, doing a routine check, when I heard this strange sound."

Brice shot a look toward Selena. She was pale, her face drained of color. After a quick shower, his mother had gotten her robe and fresh pajamas, but her hair was still damp. "I think I need to get Selena back to her room first. Mother?"

Adele hurried toward Selena. "Let's get you into bed, dear."

Selena shook her head. "No, I'm fine. I want to hear this."

Brice held up a hand. "Selena, you need to rest."

"I said I'm fine. Besides, I think I might know what Roderick is talking about." Not waiting for Brice to question that statement, she turned to Roderick. "Did this sound remind you of a bird's call or maybe a strange wailing meow?"

Roderick nodded. "Yes, ma'am, sorta. Long and piercing and downright eerie. And it was coming from inside the compound."

Selena's face went a paler shade of white. "Brice, we need to talk."

Brice's pulse pounded with the force of soldiers marching inside his brain. "First, I need to ask Roderick a few more questions." He pulled out a chair. "Selena, sit down. Mother, could you fix her a cup of tea?"

Adele went to work turning on the kettle and pulling out pie while Selena slumped in a dining chair, her head in her hands.

Brice stood with his knuckles on the bar. "Roderick, tell me why you think you did something that compromised the security system?"

Roderick squirmed and pushed at his spiky red hair. "I was doing a routine test on some of the new components you wanted installed and…well, there was a brief period this afternoon when…when the whole system went down—it just went dead on me. I hit the wrong button and the whole thing shut off."

Brice leaned into the bar, his brows lifting. "As in— we weren't secure?"

Roderick glanced at Selena then back to Brice. "Yes, sir. I mean, no, sir, we weren't secure."

"When and how long?"

Twitching, Roderick cleared his throat. "About half

an hour—mid-afternoon. But I fixed it immediately and checked the new component again and everything was fine. But while I was working on getting it back up, that's when I heard the noise. That spooky bird-call-scream-animal-like sound. When I told Dad about it, he said he'd heard the same thing the other night when he fell in the greenhouse. I checked around and I couldn't find any type of exotic bird. Do we have exotic birds on the property?"

"No, we don't," Brice said. "Where exactly did you hear this noise?"

Roderick hit his palms against the bar. Adele handed him a piece of lemon meringue pie. Shoving a forkful in his mouth, he said, "In the west garden, near the pool."

Selena glanced toward Brice. "That's just below my bedroom."

Brice exhaled a long sigh, ignoring the pie his mother placed in front of him. "I know that." He stared hard at Selena, even more sure than ever she was hiding something and pretty sure she was going to tell him everything tonight. He'd see to that. "Okay, Roderick. Thanks for leveling with me. We can fix this together. Now, off with you. Take your pie and go visit your poor mum. I'm sure she's worried sick that I'm down here throttling you."

Roderick's shoulders slumped. "I'm sorry, Brice. I was just trying to make things more secure around here. I thought I could take care of this for you. I was trying to save you some worry."

"I know you were, son. It's all right. We'll do a thorough check and get this figured out. But next time, wait for me before you shut down the entire system, okay?"

Roderick nodded. "Thanks for the pie, Miss Adele."

"You can have seconds," Adele said, her eyes gentle. Then she turned to Brice and Selena. "Eat your pie."

"I'm not hungry," they said in unison.

Selena took a tentative sip of her tea. Brice glared at the fluffy white meringue in front of him.

"You love lemon," Adele said. His mother thought pie cured everything. Between her dual Southern and Irish traditions of nurturing, no one ever went hungry around Adele Whelan. Good thing Brice worked out on a regular basis.

"I just don't have much of an appetite right now," he replied, trying to be patient. "Save mine for later."

"Mine, too," Selena said, getting up with her tea to stand by the big bay window.

"Mum, where were you and the Sagers when this happened?"

"I got home around six-thirty and decided to make this pie," Adele said. "And Betty and Charles were in their quarters watching the news. I suppose it was all over when I arrived since Roderick came straight to me with his concerns."

"Nothing out of the ordinary then?"

"Nothing I can recall. I heard the beep of an alert but Roderick came down and told me he'd had some problems. That was right after I got home and Roderick fixed it straight away."

Brice nodded. "I'll try to verify the time."

Adele looked from her son to Selena. "I guess I'll wrap this up and then turn in." She looked back at Selena. "Do you want me to call your mother to come back over?"

"No." Selena whirled, almost spilling her tea. "You two had a nice afternoon together. Don't spoil it for her. I'm okay, really. Besides it's late. I'll call her tomorrow."

The kitchen went silent after his mother discreetly left. Brice watched as Selena turned back toward the big bay window, staring out into the gardens. This place had always brought him comfort since his mother had worked hard to make parts of the estate look and feel like an Irish cottage garden. But right now, tonight, the shadows and shapes outside seemed sinister and menacing instead of beautiful and colorful. Even the moon garden, blooming in shades of alabaster, seemed to mock him, taunting him with deceptive gossamer magnolia blossoms and lush wind-tossed azalea and dogwood flowers. Who was hiding behind all that natural beauty?

He turned to stare at Selena, thinking there was a lot hiding behind her natural beauty, too. "Okay, so, you want to tell me about the bird call—or whatever that call is, luv?"

She nodded. Good. That meant she wouldn't deny it.

"I think," she said, struggling for control, struggling to look at him, "that the calls are for my benefit." She turned, sat back down. Her hands were shaking.

Brice sat beside her, taking her hands in his. "Selena, just tell me. I need to know so I can help you."

Her eyes, so luminous, so trusting, held his. "Down in Día Belo, that gang that roamed, the same gang that raided La Casa de Dios, well, they had a signal, some sort of call. I heard it a few times." She swallowed, looked down at their joined hands. "And from what Mr.

Sager described and now what Roderick described, it sounds as if this could be the same sort of signal." Pulling away, she wrapped her hands against her robe. "Brice, I think they're watching me even here at the house. And I think the calls are some sort of warning to me. I should have told you that the other night when Charles was startled, but I was afraid. And I guess I didn't want to connect the two."

"Not a warning, luv," he said, his whole system going into overdrive. "But a threat. The first time, they probably came up the river and saw a light on in the greenhouse. They sent out the call to arouse anyone who might be out there and it worked. If they managed to get inside the yard today, then that means they might have left something or someone here—to get to you." He whirled, searching for what? He couldn't begin to guess but he didn't like the sense of dread pouring over him. "The first time was a teaser. They realized you survived the bomb attack. Then they waited and when the opportunity came, they managed to sneak past our security or possibly sabotage it altogether, probably just to show us they could."

"You mean someone could be hiding out there?"

He turned back to her, saw the shock and fear on her face. And the defiance. "Yes, that's exactly what I mean." He tugged her up. "Go and sit with Roderick and his parents in their quarters. I'm going to check your room."

She grabbed his arm. "Not without me. I brought this on you, Brice."

"Do you want me to find these people?"

"Of course I do."

"Then listen to me and let me do my job. Go and stay with Roderick and the Sagers."

He pulled her through the house, not giving her time to argue. "I'll get you settled with them, then check your room. I'll be back before you know it."

"I don't want you to do this. Call someone. Call the police."

He stopped her near the back stairs. "I'm trained to do this, Selena. I don't need the police right now. Now do as I say and let's go."

She looked frightened. "I'd never forgive myself if something happened to you."

"Same here," he replied. Then he knocked on the Sagers' door and gave her a quick peck on the cheek. "I'll be fine. After all, this is my house. And in my house, I do things my way."

Which meant he'd take care of whatever interlopers he might happen to find. If it took all night and if it took all of his might.

In the meantime, he asked God to watch over Selena. That was his one prayer as he hurried to her room.

Selena tried flipping through a gardening magazine while the Sagers listened to a concert on PBS. Roderick sat at a tiny desk in the big sitting room centered between two bedrooms, his fingers tapping against a laptop.

"Do you want some more tea, Selena?" Betty asked, her bright smile too serene.

"No, thanks," Selena said, thankful for the soft chenille comforter Mrs. Sager had found for her. "I'm fine. I just wish Brice would hurry back."

Roderick stopped his tapping. "He's good at his work, Miss Selena. He'll be just fine."

"I have no doubt," Betty added. "We've always felt safe here. He's a good man."

Selena wanted to scream. While she appreciated the Sagers' quiet kindness and their admiration of Brice, she was so sick with worry she couldn't sit still. First that scene at the lake and now this. When would it end? Was she destined to live the rest of her life in fear?

Thinking about his reaction to the animal calls, she wondered why she hadn't told him the rest of her suspicions. Not just yet, she decided. She still didn't know if there was a connection between the pills she'd found on the clinic floor and all the strange things happening to her lately, but she intended to find a way to get to the bottom of her worries. But when? She'd sent the pills to be tested and she'd blurted out some of her fears to Brice tonight. What more could she do right now?

To get her mind off that, she turned to Mr. Sager. "How's your ankle, sir?"

"It's all well," Charles said with a toothy smile that reminded her of his son. "Just a little bruised, nothing more."

Roderick lifted his head again. "That strange noise sure is scary, Miss Selena. Maybe you've heard something like that in the jungle, but we don't get that kind of thing around here. I thought a panther had escaped from the Atlanta zoo or something."

A panther wouldn't be nearly as dangerous as these people, Selena thought, her mind racing with all kinds of dreadful scenarios. It didn't help that Brice was more than capable of handling the situation. She still worried for his sake. What if she lost him?

That thought caused her to draw in her breath, which

brought three sets of eyes staring at her. "Sorry," she said to the Sagers. "I'm a bit skittish."

"And no wonder," Roderick said, whirling around in his chair. "I need to tell Mr. Brice what I found. That gang you mentioned—they're pretty notorious." He stopped. "I'd better save the rest for Brice. He gets antsy if I blab too much on a case."

Selena wanted to know more, though. "I'm sure he wouldn't mind if I read over your report, Roderick."

Roderick looked toward his father. "I'd better run that by Brice first, if you don't mind."

Selena did mind, but she didn't want to get Roderick in trouble. Wondering if that report showed any indication why the Night Walkers had taken drugs from the clinic, she tried to remember what she'd seen that dark night while she was waiting for Brice. In her haste to hide, she'd grabbed the only evidence she could find—a handful of spilled pills—medication that didn't seem quite right to her. She'd never checked the locked cabinets in a back storage area but she now knew the drugs were gone. The smugglers had taken the drugs, then killed anyone who came into their path. Diego would have fought them, of that she was certain. But she needed to know why they'd come to the clinic in the first place.

Careful of how she asked the question, she looked at Roderick. "Can you at least tell me anything more about the gang?"

Roderick's Adam's apple started bobbing. "From the looks of things, they're real dangerous and they take whatever they need, including medicine and supplies. Do you think that's why they hit the clinic? That they were looking for drugs?"

Selena nodded. "That would be the obvious, wouldn't it?"

And if that were the case—that they were just looking to *sell* some drugs—any kind of drugs—then her theory could be wrong. Thankfully. Losing drugs to smugglers was bad, but not nearly as bad as what she had imagined in her head. But she still needed to validate her suspicions, one way or another. Which put her back in the position of keeping this to herself until she had conclusive results. It was the only way.

Brice would try to get enough evidence to work up a case, based on the bomb, the strange signal calls and whatever Roderick had found in that report. He'd piece it all together in the same way he did for any case. She'd keep her suspicions to herself for now. Just until Brice could get something to back what he already had.

But what if the evidence he needs is exactly what you're trying to hide? Before she could feel any remorse for even thinking that, Brice came back into the room, his expression grim.

"I think I found something," he said, his gaze lifting toward Selena. "And I think you need to see this."

ELEVEN

He practically dragged her through the dark corridors of the house. "First things first, luv." Shoving her into her bedroom, he pointed to a stuffed animal centered on the brocade comforter on the bed. "Know anything about this?"

Selena's breath hitched deep inside her diaphragm. "It's a jaguar. An endangered species in Argentina."

Brice nodded impatiently. "I know what it is. How did it get here? Did you bring it here with you?"

Selena's heart thudded and sputtered. "No." Turning to him, she added, "No, Brice, I…I didn't bring that here." She felt weak at the knees, sick with the knowledge that someone evil and nasty had invaded what she'd always considered a safe place.

"I was afraid you'd say that." Brice paced around the room, reminding her of the sleek stuffed animal lounging on her bed. "They put it here then, as another warning."

Selena sank down on the vanity stool. "Then it is real. I kept hoping—" She stopped. "Brice, I had a strange call on my cell phone a few days ago."

He stilled, standing in front of her. "Really now? And just when were you planning on mentioning this to me?"

"I'm telling you now," she said, wincing at the wrath in his dark eyes. "I tried to put it out of my mind, but—"

"Aye, *but* is right. But…now you're beginning to understand my concerns." He bent down in front of her. "Selena, this was serious from the very first shot down in Día Belo. I understood that, but apparently you didn't."

Anger brought her nose to nose with him. "I understood a lot, Brice. But I wanted to believe it would end there. Only it hasn't." Lowering her head, she said, "This hasn't been easy for me. I'm fighting for the clinic and for my life."

"Well, your life trumps the clinic hands down, so stop trying to protect it. It's too risky."

Selena understood all of the risks involved. More than he would ever realize. She opened her mouth to speak, then shut it, too quickly. Brice picked up on her hesitation.

He stood up, his hands on his hips. "Anything else you want to tell me—anything that you've been keeping from me for whatever noble reason you might have?"

She winced again. *Forgive me, Lord.* She couldn't bring herself to tell him *her* concerns. Because she couldn't be sure and she couldn't accuse anyone without being completely sure. Which meant she needed to do this on her own. Brice would rush to judgment and she couldn't risk that until she had proof. Then she'd have no choice; she'd have to go to the authorities. "That's the only other thing that's happened since the bombing—

but with the strange signal calls and the phone call… well…I can't keep denying that this is real."

"Oh, you can bet it's real. They're taunting you. The bomb didn't work but they mean to make you sweat. And they're out there, waiting for another opportunity."

"What if someone *is* out there—I mean here on the estate, hiding?" she asked, jumping up to glance at the closed drapery. "There are all kinds of places to hide around here."

"Aye, tell me." He pushed at his shaggy bangs. "I've walked the property and found footprints and I'll have Roderick help me check for any activity on the security cameras, but they probably came right inside when the system went down. I've called in reinforcements. You remember my friend Vern Edwards?"

She lifted her chin. "Big, burly bodyguard type. I remember how he used to hover around when I came to visit."

"Well, he'll be back, hovering around again. I've called him home from a fishing expedition for extra security. And I've also contacted the Knight."

"The Knight?" Selena touched at the drapery. "Your friend Shane?"

He nodded. "Friend and special investigator. He deals in foreign espionage for CHAIM. He might have some input on these smugglers since he travels in international circles."

Selena swallowed, fear clawing at her nerves. "Shane Warwick is coming here from England to help you?"

"Yes, luv." He touched a hand to her hair, his golden-green eyes roving over her face. "I seem to have lost my perspective on this. I'm too close."

"Because of me?"

He moved toward her, his gaze locking with hers. "Well, yes. If I hadn't been so keen on making sure you didn't set off on your own every waking hour—the way you inadvertently did at the lake today—I would have realized that what my staff has been describing is not a bird call at all."

"What do you mean?"

"It's the call of a jaguar, darlin'. Better known as *yaguareté* or *yaguar* in Argentina, I believe. This sound everyone's been describing isn't a purr or a roar, but a loud kind of mew or growl. A big cat's coughing mew in the dead of night. I hope to hear it on the surveillance video but our friends have been clever. They probably made sure nothing showed up there. Obviously the Night Walkers have adopted this call to meet their nocturnal purposes. But I think you knew all of this already, didn't you, since you recognized the call."

Selena saw the hurt and frustration in his eyes. "I knew about the Night Walkers. Everyone in the village knows about them and I told you I was pretty sure they were the ones who hit the clinic. But up until now, they've never bothered the clinic. They deal in illegal goods, but I didn't think they dealt in drugs—especially prescription drugs. That's not their style." Or at least she hoped that wasn't their style.

He hit a fist against the back of a cushioned chair. "Selena, how could you not suspect that? These people raided your clinic. Isn't that the obvious thing—that they'd be after drugs? I'd think the drug cabinet would have been the first place they'd go."

"I didn't give it much thought at the time, Brice. I

was too busy trying to hide—trying to save my own life."

He put his hands on her shoulders, forcing her to look him in the eye. "Or maybe you were too afraid—you said so yourself. Too afraid to tell me that your boyfriend Diego might be involved in some sort of drug smuggling operation and that operation went bad? Is that it, Selena?"

She wished it was that easy to explain. "Diego wasn't like that. I knew him. He was a good doctor and he was a Christian. He'd never become involved in anything illegal."

Would he? Trying to push that question away, she said, "He died trying to help the villagers, Brice. He put himself between them and the smugglers. I should have helped. I should have tried to do more."

"You did the only thing you could. You got there too late and it was over. Hiding was your best option."

"But…why me? Why did I survive?"

"I can't explain that," he replied, his scowl softening. "But if we're not careful, you might not survive now. These people have no scruples—they've been very bold so far. They won't stop until they finish the job. They must think you saw something or someone, so they need to eliminate you." He took one of her hands in his, the warmth of his fingers moving over her knuckles like the soft fibers of a comfortable blanket. "So now would be a good time to tell me everything— anything you can remember or anything you think you might know. Starting with the drug supply."

She should do just that, but something held her back. Brice would not take her suspicions lightly—he'd go right to Dr. Jarrell and interrogate the poor man. And until she had solid proof, she couldn't allow that. It would only add to her humiliation and her pain. Somehow, she had to prove that Diego didn't die in vain and that her mentor, the man she'd trusted since birth, the doctor who'd watched with pride as she'd become an R.N., hadn't betrayed her.

"I only know that they did take drugs. Dr. Jarrell confirmed that. I'm sure they slipped them out of the country, probably in—" She turned away, staring at the plush stuffed animal on the bed.

Brice followed her gaze, then grabbed the toy. Before she could blink, he pulled out a pocket knife and slit the furry creature's stomach open. Pills of all colors spilled out from the torn plastic bag shoved inside the animal.

Selena's heart palpitated so fast her stomach clenched. "Why would they leave this here?"

"To scare you," he said. "More threats." Grabbing a tissue from the nightstand, he carefully pushed the pills back inside the tattered bag. "We need to have these analyzed." Then he turned to face her. "Unless you can explain what kind of drugs these are?"

Selena stared at the multicolored pills. "With the various shapes and sizes, it looks like a variety of what we supplied in the on-site pharmacy."

"Who was in charge of the pharmacy?"

"Diego," she said. "But we had a trained assistant and an on-site pharmacist to help inventory and distribute the meds. They both died in the raid." And she wondered for the hundredth time if either of them had been involved.

"Anything else? Think, Selena. Did Diego or

anyone else connected with the clinic ever mention the Night Walkers?"

"Not that I can remember. We were all aware of them, of course, but they were never mentioned as a threat to the clinic." At his skeptical look, she added, "I've told you everything I know to be the truth, Brice. Maybe they needed something else to sell on the black market and we were an easy target. Diego and the villagers stumbled in on that, so they killed all the witnesses."

"All except one," Brice said, his tone a low growl. "All except you, luv." He picked up the torn plush jaguar. "I'll take this and have it checked for prints, at least. Although I'm sure they didn't leave anything behind except what they wanted to leave."

Selena got up. "Which means *me,* for now."

"Yes, that means you—until they try to finish the job. I can't let that happen."

But how could he keep that from happening? she wondered. Next time, they might just find her and take her. She should tell him the rest of her fears. But what did it matter now? They both knew she was being targeted by the Night Walkers. And that's what Brice would focus on—keeping her safe. Which meant he'd go after anyone he suspected, including Dr. Jarrell. That could be disastrous.

"For now, we keep watch," he echoed, his eyes golden in the lamplight. "Will you be able to sleep?"

"I hope so." She nodded toward the balcony. "They can't get in here again, right?"

"Not anymore. I'll make sure of that with extra security. My mother is right next door and I'm just down the hall. There are sensors on the balcony railings and all along the windows and doors, but they obviously slipped through when the system went down." He ran a hand through his hair. "And now I'm thinking that was no accident. Roderick blames himself, but I think someone else managed to knock out our system just long enough to wreak havoc."

"And get into my room."

He nodded. "I checked everything else. They didn't take anything."

Thankful that the pills she'd found were no longer hidden in her tote bag, Selena breathed a sigh of relief. Several of them were being analyzed and the rest she'd hidden at the clinic.

Brice came to stand in front of her. "Roderick and I will check the security again to be sure the system is intact. One touch and this place will light up like a Christmas tree and alarms will sound very loudly." He leaned toward her, his intent as catlike and stealthy as the jaguar he held in one hand. Lifting her chin with his other hand, he tugged her close. "And besides, I won't be sleeping. So you can rest for the both of us." He leaned close, his lips brushing hers in the lightest of kisses. Then he quoted Shakespeare. "'Is it thy will, thy image should keep open my heavy eyelids to the weary night?'"

Selena leaned her forehead against his, savoring his touch. "You don't have to stay awake for me, Brice."

"Aye, but I do, luv. I truly do."

With that, he lifted his head, gave her a bittersweet smile and left her standing at the door, cold and alone once again.

* * *

Roderick was waiting for Brice in his downstairs office. "I've found more information, Brice."

Brice stared silently up at Roderick's expectant face. "Good work. Is there something else you want to say?"

Roderick clutched the papers in his hands. "I guess I'm toast, huh?"

Scowling, Brice lifted his head. "Toast?"

"Fired. Done for. Going up the river or back to Ireland." Roderick's ruddy cheeks flared like a bushfire. "I really blew it when I turned off the security system, didn't I?"

Brice wanted to grab the boy by his polo shirt collar and tell him in no uncertain terms that yes, he had really messed up. But he didn't have the heart to do that. The young man was just that—a young man. And he was trying so hard to live up to CHAIM standards, much in the same way Brice had tried to do when he'd first started out.

"We all make mistakes," Brice said, wondering why he couldn't muster up something more original as a lesson.

"But this was a big one," Roderick replied. "I should have asked your permission. I mean, this is why you're calling Vern back, right? And that Camelot person—Sir Warwick. I can't do the job, so you called in real agents."

Brice's face muscles hurt from the soft smile breaking through. He hadn't had a whole lot to smile about recently. "Shane? He's not exactly from Camelot, Rod, but that is one of his favorite musicals and yes, he was knighted by the Queen of England." Shaking his head, he added, "I'm calling other people in because, frankly, I think we're both in over our heads. I know what to do and how to do it—I've handled lots of cases involving threatened missionaries in third world countries, but this case is different. This is Selena. And I'm losing my perspective. I need fresh eyes and more objective minds, understand?"

Roderick's Adam's apple bobbed. "I think I do. You care too much?"

"Aye, I care too much. Too very much. And Roderick, I still need your help, too." He templed his hands on the desk. "Because, lad, I'm not so sure the security breach was all your fault."

"Really?"

Brice nodded. "I'm thinking maybe someone was just waiting and watching for the right moment to strike. They did this while I was away."

Roderick's eyes went wide. "That sure makes sense. Why didn't I see that?"

"You'll learn. And so will I. I left thinking our security was tight. I was wrong."

Roderick hit a hand on his head. "Oh, I meant to show you this, too." He turned to the computer. "I pulled up the surveillance video for the river, both today's and that of the night my dad heard that weird noise. Watch this."

Brice watched the tapes, his thoughts grim. A dark boat moved just near the right upper screen. "They drove a boat right up to the river," he said, watching the tapes over again. "Just out of reach of our cameras."

Roderick nodded. "I can't get a fix on what kind of boat except that it had to be a speed boat. They probably paddled away, then took off."

Something about that nagged at Brice, but he was too tired to make a connection. "What else?" He motioned for the kid to hand him the report. After glancing over it, he pulled a hand down his jaw. "This confirms what we already knew. They're smugglers by trade but they've only been connected to illegal weapons and domestic items such as apparel and shoes, purses and jewelry. So why did they take drugs from the clinic?"

Roderick sank down in a chair. "Something new to sell?"

Selena had suggested that—or had she pointed it out to throw him off? Brice's heart hurt, knowing she didn't trust him enough to tell him everything. What would motivate her to keep information from him?

Only one thing. She was definitely trying to protect someone. Diego was dead—not much need to protect him now. But Dr. Jarrell was very much alive. Why did Brice keep coming back to the good doctor? Would Selena deliberately protect the man, even if she knew he was involved in something highly illegal? He couldn't imagine that. Selena was too honest for that kind of risk.

Roderick sat straight up. "What if someone at the clinic offered to sell them drugs? You know, to make some extra money." He tapped his fingers on the desk. "Missionaries don't get paid much, if at all, right?"

"Right." Brice looked back at the files. "I can understand pain pills, but standard drugs such as antibiotics or specialty drugs—those wouldn't serve very well on the black market. I'll talk to Selena about this again first thing tomorrow." If he could get her to talk. She shut down each time he mentioned Diego and the drug cabinet. And each time she shut down, Brice's radar went into a warning blast inside his mind.

"Do you think one of the clinic workers was some sort of…druggie or double agent?"

Impressed with Roderick's excitement and persistence, Brice could only nod. "Anything is possible. But… if they had someone working inside, they would have been more subtle." He looked up at the kid as they both came to the same conclusion.

"Unless that someone had double-crossed the gang," Roderick said, his bristling hair seeming to stand up on his head. "Think that's it?"

Brice nodded again. "I've wondered that at times, yes." And that would explain why Selena was being so cryptic. If her precious Diego had been dealing in prescription drugs and had suddenly decided to end it, the Night Walkers would have retaliated in the only way they knew. With brute force. And that might be why Selena wasn't talking. She wanted to protect the clinic and the villagers because she wanted to return to her work there. If there were any hint of illegal activities, CHAIM would shut the clinic down forever, with her formidable father, Delton Carter, leading the charge.

That brought him back to Dr. Jarrell. The man had almost single-handedly set up the clinic. He didn't know CHAIM was one of the major supporters since all of their funding had gone through Delton Carter. But the doctor would work very hard to cover any discrepancies or unethical activities and Selena would certainly want to protect Dr. Jarrell.

Which left Brice still wondering and waiting. He'd

have to make her talk, one way or another. And he couldn't use his usual mode of harsh interrogation—not on Selena.

He was tired and he was worried, but he was also Irish. He'd try a new tack on Selena.

He'd woo the information out of her. And while he was at it, he'd woo her heart, too. Might as well make the best of a bad situation. After all, he was holding her captive, so to speak.

And it was high time the lady of the tower let down her hair and told him all of her heart's secrets. Not only to bring her closer, but to possibly save her life.

Selena's cell phone rang. Glancing at the clock, she swallowed back panic. The last time she'd received a late night message, it had been a threat. Why was she doing this? Did she think she could hold out vital information until these people went away? Or was she trying to hold out because she always took care of herself and she wanted to do that this time, too?

Relieved to see her mother's number on the caller ID, she slumped back against the bed. "Hello," she said, her voice low and shaky.

"Darlin', it's Mother. Adele called me and told me what happened at the lake. I wanted to see how you're doing."

"Oh," Selena said, glad to hear her mother's voice but not the message. "I'm fine. I told her not to worry you."

"I'm your mother, darlin'. Worry is my middle name. I've decided I'm not going to join your father in Chicago. He just needs a few more days there anyway."

"You don't need to stay home for me," Selena said. "Brice is making sure I'm safe." She didn't dare tell her mother about the stuffed animal they'd found on her bed.

"I believe that, but I don't want to leave just now."

"Mother, please go and be with Daddy. I'll be the one worried. This way, I'll know you're out of the city and protected."

"While you're a sitting duck?"

"I'm fine," Selena said. "Brice is working hard to end this. Go and be with Daddy and don't worry about me."

Bea sighed long and hard. "You promise you'll stay right there with Brice and Adele. Your father doesn't want you traveling too far from that house."

"I can see his reasoning," Selena said, trembling in spite of the night light by her bed. "I'll behave and mind Brice, okay? And we can keep in touch. I'll call you every day."

"You'd better, honey. Your father will be up to his eyeballs in CHAIM meetings and I can't help but worry. But Brice will take care of you, I have no doubt."

If I let him, Selena thought.

As if reading her thoughts, Bea said, "Honey, listen to Brice. Your father would have never left Atlanta if he thought Brice couldn't handle this. Trust him, and trust God in all things."

"You're right," Selena said, tears pricking her eyes. "I love you both. Tell Daddy that for me. And tell him not to worry. I'm fine." She hoped.

"Of course, sugah. Now the house is locked up tight and I've got the security company on patrol, so don't worry about that. Just stay safe. I'll call you first thing tomorrow."

"You promise?"

"Of course," Bea said, her tone reassuring. "Get some rest."

Selena hung up, wondering how she'd be able to rest now. The room shouted a silent warning to her, making her wish for someone to run to, someone in which to confide all of her worries and fears. Should she find Brice?

What should I do, Lord? I'm not used to asking for help. True, she always turned to God, but then it was easy to send out prayers of faith. Why couldn't she do the same with Brice? Why couldn't she just go on faith with her feelings for him and with her need to be honest with him?

Because you think that's a sign of weakness, she admitted to herself. "Silly me." Touching a hand to her Bible, she asked God to protect her parents.

And help me to be honest with Brice.

Before she knew it, Selena had taken a quick shower, then put on a T-shirt and some comfortable jeans. She had to talk to Brice. Thinking about all the things that could go wrong only reinforced her own vulnerability. And before, Brice had always been the one she turned to when she needed to talk. Maybe that was why she'd called him that horrible day when she returned to the village to find everyone dead and a band of renegades still sneaking around. Because Brice always knew what to say or what to do.

Only this time, the stakes were high. Too high for her to just blurt out her suspicions and worries without any proof. Brice knew about the Night Walkers; he knew about their secret night call. And he also knew they'd followed her here and sent her some very pointed warnings. That's all anyone knew for sure.

But she had to talk to someone. She was halfway

down the long upstairs hallway to Brice's office when she stopped. Maybe she should talk to Dr. Jarrell again before she said anything else to Brice. Dr. Jarrell would know what to do. Then she could go to Brice with an open heart and a big burden off her chest, at least.

That's what she'd do. She'd tell Dr. Jarrell that she was afraid Diego had been dealing in counterfeit prescription drugs and that some of those drugs might have filtered here to Atlanta.

Dr. Jarrell would help her investigate and together, they'd report their findings. Before someone else died.

TWELVE

Selena stared at the computer screen, then glanced over her shoulder to make sure no one was behind her. The drug analysis had come back—or rather the *fake* drug report had come back. Mr. Cooper's Digoxin was made mostly of talcum powder and other dust, same as the handful of pills she'd saved from the clinic floor. Nothing but toxins and dust in all of them. She read the words over again, her eyes scanning all the scientific names to get to the essence of the report. Possible combination of chalk, wheat flour or turmeric.

Mr. Cooper had died from taking medicine that didn't contain anything to help his heart. And what about the woman who'd died right here the day Brice had come to the clinic? She'd been taking the same medicine.

Selena saved the document in her personal files then sank down on her chair, her head in her hands. All along, she'd been worried about this but she'd convinced herself the gang had targeted the clinic looking for drugs to sell. But what if the Night Walkers had come to the clinic to seek revenge because someone there had figured out they were helping the clinic traffic in counterfeit prescription drugs—drugs every bit as dangerous as the worst heroin or crack? And how was she going to tell Dr. Jarrell this?

She'd tried to find some quiet time all day to talk to him again but that had been near impossible. They were always surrounded by either patients or coworkers. She had to tell him now. This was illegal and life-threatening. The Food and Drug Administration would have to be notified. They'd want to order even more toxicology reports. And the FDA would immediately shut down the clinic.

Dear Lord, help me, she silently prayed. *What's going on here? Who's responsible?* And how long had this been happening right under her nose? Maybe, she thought, maybe no one actually knew they'd been prescribing counterfeit drugs. Maybe Diego wasn't involved but someone here at Haven Center had to be. Maybe, maybe, maybe. Those bandits had known something, had come searching the clinic for something or someone. Her head ricocheted with a booming pulse each time she tried to think past what she'd read on that report.

Then she remembered the threatening phone call. "You have something we want."

Did someone know she'd taken pills as evidence? And that voice—why did it sound vaguely familiar to her now?

"Selena, you said you needed to speak with me?"

She whirled around to find Dr. Jarrell at the door. How could she tell him when she didn't know who was involved in this? Did he know? Or was he as clueless as she'd been?

He gave her a laser stare through his bifocals. "Selena, dear, are you all right?"

She stood up, steadying herself against the shock still humming throughout her system. She had no choice. She had an ethical duty to report this now that her suspicions had been confirmed. "I'm concerned about something I found at the clinic, right after the raid. I think the same thing is happening here now— remember I talked to you about this at the lake? We have a problem with our meds. I've confirmed it."

He stepped into the room and shut the door. "What are you talking about?"

Selena quickly explained, then pulled up the toxicology report. "We have to notify the authorities."

Dr. Jarrell looked as upset as she felt. He went pale then leaned against the door, his hands gripping the inside of his lab coat pockets. "I can't believe this. Why didn't you come to me sooner? You didn't tell me about this the other day—that you'd actually requested a toxicology report."

Selena looked down at the papers on her desk. "Don't worry. I went to a discreet friend at a drug testing lab—it's all anonymous at this point. I wanted to be sure before I accused anyone and I just now got the report back. But considering we receive most of our drug supplies for both clinics through an Internet site, it stands to reason our meds could easily be switched or tampered with. I pray I'm wrong and Diego wasn't involved." She took a long breath. "And…it means someone here could be involved, too."

His eyes went dark as his skin changed from washed-out pale to livid red. "Have you told anyone else about your suspicions?"

"No," she said. "I first suspected it when the clinic was hit. I found some pills that looked suspicious. Then after Mr. Cooper died…it just didn't make sense. I had to know the truth before I could accuse anyone. But I haven't even told Brice about my concerns."

He let out a sigh. "Let's keep it that way for now."

"But—"

Dr. Jarrell pushed off the wall, then surprised Selena by putting his hands on her arms, both his tone and expression bordering on frantic. "Let me take care of this, Selena. You've been through so much. I'll report your findings and see what else we have to do. I hope this doesn't mean we'll have to shut down the Haven Center, but it might come to that."

"I know," she said, backing up to stare at him. "That's my worst fear. But better that than causing our patients any harm. We've lost two so far from this, based on the meds they were taking. I can't let that happen again."

"Of course. Print me out a copy of the toxicology report and we'll go from there. We'll have to have some more samples tested, but this time we'll make it official. *I'll* report it myself and we'll have a proper lab handle it from here on out."

Feeling chastised, Selena quickly did as he asked, handing him the paper. Then she told him about the other threats—the phone call and the nocturnal signal calls as well as the stuffed animal, including the pills Brice had found there. "He's having those pills tested. I couldn't stop him. I'm so sorry."

"I am, too," the doctor said, scowling. "And I'm very disappointed that you didn't come to me immediately. This could ruin us for good."

They could certainly agree on that, but she didn't need him to remind her that she'd stalled too long. Her father would be devastated and disappointed in her, too. "I think I need to tell Brice," she said, wishing she'd done that from the very first day. At the doctor's disapproving frown, she added, "Brice can be objective and professional. He doesn't have a personal stake in this. He can help us figure out who's behind this."

"Yes, but he's also a hothead. His actions at the lake prove that. We need to keep this low key or he might just turn vigilante and cause us a lot of problems, especially if he gets back his own report on the stashed pills before we can make a move." The doctor studied her for a minute, then said, "Give me until the morning, Selena. I've got a lot invested in this clinic. We'll need to immediately recall all the suspected meds and shut down the on-site pharmacy. In fact, I'll start calling patients and ask them to come in and bring their medication first thing tomorrow."

"I can help with that," she offered.

"No, you go home. I insist. I'll get Meg or one of the interns to help. I just need you to keep a lid on this until I can get my thoughts together. So go home and stay close to Brice, in case he's found out something else. And if he hears back on that report, call me with the findings."

Selena saw the anxiety in his eyes. "We can't reopen the Día Belo clinic until all of this is cleared up. And now, we might have to shut down this clinic, too. I hate this."

"I do, too, but we can't risk patients becoming ill or dying because of bad medication. We'll get through this investigation, Selena, and then we'll get on with our work.

And we'll find the people who threatened you. It seems our Diego was involved in illegal activities, after all."

She put her hands across her midsection. "We don't know it was him for sure, but it looks that way. I really think it's time to alert Brice on this. I've already kept this to myself for days now. I don't feel comfortable keeping it from Brice, now that I have proof."

Dr. Jarrell put his arms on her shoulders again. "I understand, dear, but please let me handle this. He's protecting *you,* but this is my concern. And you only had a few pills analyzed. Plus, you didn't follow proper procedure. Let me do a bit more checking. I'll go through the correct channels, I promise."

Feeling incompetent for not following protocol, she asked, "Should I go with you—I mean, shouldn't we report this together?"

"No, no. I'm going to call a board meeting for tomorrow morning and, of course, the FDA Office of Criminal Investigations will immediately launch a full investigation. But first, I'll decide how best to proceed. In the meantime, I suggest you go home and get a good night's rest. Let me worry about this for a while." He turned at the door. "Just trust me."

Selena busied herself with closing down her computer after Dr. Jarrell left the room, her mind racing with all the possibilities. Had she done the right thing, going to him first? Someone in this clinic had to know what was going on. Who was it?

"Hey, ready to go home?"

An hour had gone by since Selena's talk with Dr. Jarrell. She turned to stare up at Brice, shock and guilt merging like a fast-moving river inside her beating heart. "Uh…yes. I mean, not yet."

He immediately went on high alert, his eyebrows lifting, his jaw muscles tightening. "What's wrong? I saw Dr. Jarrell come in here and shut the door."

Selena brushed at her ponytail, then averted her eyes, wishing her facial expressions didn't give her away so much. "Nothing. I mean, we were just discussing a patient. And after he left, I was just so immersed in my reports, you scared me."

"You had another busy day," Brice said, jutting a hip on the corner of the cluttered desk, his presence filling the small office. He leaned close, the scent of spicy aftershave wafting around him. "But I'm here to take you away from all of this."

"Oh, really?" She looked up at him, seeing the sincerity and confidence in his eyes. "I'm not so sure—"

"I am. We're going to have a nice dinner, luv. And I won't take no for an answer."

"But I thought I couldn't go out anymore, except to work and back." At least that had been the routine over the past couple of days after he'd found the stuffed animal on her bed.

"That's specific and still is, but we've had extra security all around my house and here at the clinic. We'll be dining in, but in the solarium and alone—I've sent Mum and the Sagers out for a nice relaxing movie and dinner on me. And we'll have Vern for a bodyguard. Don't worry. You'll be safe."

"I know I'm safe with you," she said, managing a smile. "I'm just surprised that you're offering this, I mean, since the incident the other night."

His face darkened at that reminder. "The jaguar? That happened because of the security shutdown. Roderick has been seriously reprimanded even though I have my doubts it was entirely his fault, but we've beefed things up. It won't happen again. And since I was kind of harsh about that, I thought I could make it up to you."

Selena thought that was a lovely sentiment, but she wasn't in the mood. Her mind was all jumbled with old doubts and new revelations—and keeping this from him yet again. "I'm kinda tired."

His eyes held a determined glint. "All you have to do when we get home is change into the dress you'll find on your bed. Now that's not so hard, is it?"

"You've thought of everything." She hesitated, but decided if she couldn't tell him what she'd found, at least they'd have a private place to talk. Besides, she had to think about what to do next. Who could she trust?

She could trust Brice. And she couldn't hide this from him any longer. She'd tell him her findings tonight at dinner and ask him to keep it quiet until Dr. Jarrell had alerted the authorities. She'd be alone with Brice and it might prove easier to open up after a good meal. If she could even eat. "I think I can manage to freshen up and change," she finally said. "Thanks for planning this. I could use a change of pace."

"Exactly," Brice said, his grin a small reward. The man's smile could make flowers bloom. "Tonight, we'll forget all of this for just a couple of hours. And not to worry, I've got people on the case so this investigation hasn't shut down. *We're* just taking a break until Shane finishes his investigation and gets here, hopefully, late tonight or tomorrow."

A break. That's exactly what she needed, exactly what Dr. Jarrell had asked for—just some time. And the doctor would do the right thing. He'd make sure his patients were unharmed. "Sounds great. Just let me get my things."

Selena watched as Brice lifted off the desk. "I'll be just outside," he said with a salute.

She nodded, anticipation pushing at her guilt and her need to confess all. It was time to come clean, at last.

Brice hoped he'd smiled enough to convince Selena. He wasn't one for duplicity but desperate men did desperate things. And he was desperate to get her to open up to him. He knew he was almost there; he'd come close to putting all the pieces together. But something was missing, something big and glaring and right in front of his eyes.

He'd realized this when Shane had called earlier, declaring that Día Belo seemed to be a direct route for certain kinds of trafficking.

"I took a thorough walking tour of the entire area down there. It's centered near three rivers and the border with Brazil, Brice. That area is known for trafficking and smuggling. It's a very dangerous area, a hotbed of terrorists and international criminals. Beautiful but dangerous, much like my last relationship."

"But we knew that going in, and so did you in your last failed relationship, if I remember correctly," Brice reminded him, used to Shane's wry wit. "That's one of the reasons CHAIM set up a mission and clinic there. We were hoping to help people."

"Oh, we've been a strong presence in the village, but

someone got greedy, I think," Shane countered in his curt British accent. "But it's not what you'd expect. That report you ordered—it's come back. But I want to be sure before…we discuss it. Also, watch out for the *intern*." Then he'd quoted Scripture. *But we will go along by the king's highway, until we be past thy borders.*

Numbers 21. Borders. Brice could figure out the rest. Someone was smuggling prescription drugs over the border—in this case over international borders. So this was big, very big. And that term "highway" meant this stuff was out on the streets everywhere. Meaning Atlanta, too, probably. Also meaning that a criminal mastermind was probably behind this, someone powerful *and* nasty—never a good mix. And what did Gregory Gordon, the intern Shane referenced, have to do with this?

Shane had refused to elaborate over the phone. "I'll be there within the next twelve hours, give or take, to compare notes and see what we can do. Just be careful and try to get your client to talk."

Brice imagined that "give or take" meant Shane was doing some more extensive research along the way. And if anyone could sneak in and out of a place unde-tected—even wearing a tuxedo and a killer smile—it would be the suave, ultra-cool Shane Warwick.

So in the meantime, Brice went back to his own plan "to get the client to talk." He wanted to show Selena that he could be trusted and he also wanted to show her that he could make her happy. A double assignment, cloaked in soft music, candlelight and sweet words whispered in her ear. That part would be easy—he'd done this routine a hundred times over. But with Selena, that part would not be a deception, He needed to whisper sweet words in her ear. He needed her to see that he was in love with her. Had always been in love with her. The hard part would be making her see that she needed to confide in him—no matter what.

Selena stared at herself in the mirror, wondering why she was dressed to the nines when her life was slowly unraveling and trailing like a jungle vine. How could she relax and enjoy being with Brice with all these secrets hanging over her head? And how can I find out the truth?

A knock at her door told her Brice was ready to take her down to dinner. Her heart fluttered like one of the thousands of butterflies she used to marvel at in the rain forest. Caught between a grudging deception and a longing to let her heart takes its own course, Selena closed her eyes for a brief prayer. *What should I do, Lord? How can I reconcile all the fears and doubts inside my heart?*

She should not wear a cloak of fear, Selena reminded herself. She'd had the courage to go down to Argentina, to fight for those villagers who lived in such a volatile area of the world, but why hadn't she been able to save them when they needed her the most?

The knock sounded a second time. "Selena?"

"Coming," she called, the shimmer of her green dress cascading around her legs as she walked to the door. Wiping her palms together, she inhaled a deep breath, then swung the door open, her gaze locking with Brice's.

His eyes went wide, the cascading shades of yellow and green inside his irises shimmering as he looked her over. "Beautiful," he said on a whisper of breath. "'Tread softly because you tread on my dreams.'"

Yeats. He certainly was pulling out all the stops.

"Thank you." Selena pivoted, her pulse quickening. "Your mother has exquisite taste in clothes."

"It's not the dress, it's the woman wearing it," Brice replied.

To take the edge off her hammering heart, Selena waved a hand toward him. "You don't look too shabby either."

He touched the bow tie at his throat. "It was worth the tux just to see you in that dress, luv."

She grabbed a white silk wrap and her cell phone. At Brice's questioning look, she said, "In case my mother calls. She'll panic if I don't answer."

"Ah, you're right."

As he closed the door behind her, she said, "I don't see why we had to get all gussied up for dinner since we're not leaving the house." She was glad they were staying in, but she kept that to herself.

Brice took her wrap and gently placed it around her bare shoulders. "Maybe just so I could see you in this dress, hmm?"

She smiled at that. "It has been a while since I wore such a lovely dress—probably not since Cotillion."

He stopped on the landing. "I remember that night. You were a princess on the court, and a princess in my heart, even if your escort was the college quarterback— and a regular *ijit*." He shrugged. "Or maybe I was the idiot, letting him hang all over you."

"You're so full of blarney," she said, suddenly shy. "But I love you anyway."

She heard the intake of his breath before she felt it warm and tickling on her neck. "Do you…love me, I mean?"

What to say? "Of course I do. You know that." She managed a little laugh to waylay the implications of that pledge. "You're the best friend a girl could ever have."

He took her elbow, his eyes going as blank and heavy as the drapery surrounding the arched window covering the entire landing. "Aye, that I am. And a fairly decent bodyguard, too, right? An all-around good guy."

"Yes." She swallowed back the words trapped in the haze of her heart. "Although I haven't been the best of clients."

"You are rather a handful, but worth the effort."

Selena lowered her head as they reached the wide foyer downstairs. She wanted to be worthy—of both Brice and of God's redeeming love. She'd tried so hard to give her life to the Lord by serving Him. When she'd first told her parents she wanted to be a missionary, they'd both blanched. But Delton Carter had come from a long line of adventurers and philanthropists so he'd finally caved and allowed her to follow her heart, provided she always knew she could come back home.

But she never dreamed she'd come back to Atlanta under a cloud of fear and suspicion. "Any more information?" she asked Brice as he escorted her toward the solarium at the back of the house. "Did you find out about the pills?"

"Nothing we need to discuss tonight, luv," he retorted. "I'm still waiting on the official report from Shane."

And for the first time Selena saw something mirrored there inside his eyes, something that she recognized deep inside her soul—a deliberate avoidance that seemed almost like a deception. And she had to wonder—did he already know all of her closely guarded secrets?

THIRTEEN

They sat inside the solarium with the doors thrown open to the garden beyond. The music of Brahms played in the background, as precise and timeless as the stars and the moon. The scent of a thousand flowers wafted over them—orchids, roses, lilies and jasmine in a garden sweet and lush with floral perfumes, alive and illuminated by the twinkling stars and the glow of the city skyline in the distance just beyond the trees. The lingering fragrance of Adele's rare orchid cactus smelled like vanilla and lived up to its name of "Queen of the Night." The sound of night birds and frogs called out in a constant lullaby. And the nearby lily pond glistened like a bowl of liquid crystal in the spilled moonlight filtering through the ancient magnolia and oak trees.

"This is so perfect."

Selena hoped the catch in her voice wouldn't turn into a full-fledged crying jag. But she wanted to cry from the sheer beauty of this night, coupled with the exhaustion of keeping her wits and her secrets intact. "Brice, how did you know to bring me here to the solarium?"

   The man sitting across the table from her inside the glass-walled room smiled his slow dazzling smile and shrugged as he reached for her hand. "I wanted you to feel as if you were back near the rain forest. I couldn't bring the waterfalls and tropical foliage from your beloved village to you, so I brought you to the next best place—a table with a view of my mum's garden."

   Selena pushed at her dessert—fresh strawberries and cream over a flaky shortcake. "This was so thoughtful—dinner just for us. I didn't realize how much I missed the rain forest until we walked into this room tonight." She closed her eyes. "I remember the butterflies, thousands of them, and the sound of the falls—it was constant and always so reassuring. It renewed my faith. I knew only God could have created something so beautiful." Holding his hand tightly against hers, she said, "Thank you so much."

   "No big deal. My mum is an avid gardener but I rarely take the time to enjoy her efforts or those of the Sagers and our staff." Brice stood, then lifted her hand. "Would you like to dance?"

   Selena nodded, aware that Vern Edwards stood nearby, keeping watch near the open doors, along with a specially hired security guard making the rounds on the perimeter of the property, so she and Brice could enjoy this reprieve. Vern was six feet tall with the shoulders of an ox. Brice had hinted of his training—everything from the Marines to DEA to CHAIM, Vern had seen it or done it. She felt secure with him here.

   But she felt even safer as Brice took her in his arms and held her close, swaying in a waltz as they twirled around the enclosed cocoon of the large glass-walled room. As the music stopped so did he. But he didn't let her go. He just stood with her close in his arms, his gaze holding hers in a silent, eloquent recital that told of long-held feelings and so little time to reveal them. The nearby fountain's cascading water managed to hide the sudden rush of her pulse as he looked down into her eyes.

"Selena, I brought you here for a reason."

She nodded, her sigh shuddering out of her body as if the night breeze had touched on her very soul, her thoughts full of relief mixed with trepidation. "You want me to talk to you, don't you? You need me to tell you everything and I want to tell you. You know me that well."

He seemed surprised and embarrassed. "Yes, I know you that well. And I'm concerned, very concerned."

She smiled, her hand going to his face, her fingers tracing the smooth skin of his jaw. "So you figured you'd show me your romantic side, to get me in the mood to spill my secrets? That must come in handy for some of your CHAIM assignments, but I've never quite seen this side of you, not in the way many women have, I'm sure. But I've always wondered what would happen if you let go and turned that Irish charm on full force. And now I know."

His astonished gaze moved over her face, his eyes full of wonder. "Do you now? Are you sure you truly know *me?*"

She shook her head. "I thought I knew my friend and the man who traveled around the world to help me. But you're the one who's been holding back, Brice. You're the one who wasn't so willing to open up *to me.*"

He chuckled but it was nervous with a new awareness. "Don't go turning the tables on me, *cara*. You have always held my heart open and waiting in your hands."

"But you've never given all of *your* heart over to me—not completely," she replied, the hurt of his necessary charms cutting through her soul. "Because of CHAIM and your duty to your job. And you won't tonight, not until you know everything you need to know. Am I right? Is that the price then? A trade, a fair swap of information?"

He stepped back, his expression a cross between a scowl and a smile. "I just want to protect you, but I think you're trying so hard to protect someone else that you're afraid to trust me. Even me, Selena? Don't you know you can trust me with everything—including *your* heart?"

"I do," she said, a long-held breath escaping. "And I do need to tell you something." She leaned up, kissed him square on the lips, then whispered, "But you didn't have to ply me with all of this. I had decided today that I needed to talk to you. No more secrets or doubts."

He pulled her close, his scowl easing away, his expression changing to awe and acceptance, laced with that constant concern. "You mean I wasted a perfectly good spring night and all this charm for nothing?"

Selena playfully slapped him on the arm, willing to forgive him for setting her up in such a calculatingly sweet way. It had helped calm her wired nerves even though he'd used a bit of trickery to do it. "Nothing was wasted here, Brice Whelan. You knew exactly what you were doing." Then she kissed him again just so she could have a memory of this moment before she told him what she'd found out today. "You win. We need to have a very long talk. But…I'm glad we had this night before that talk, at least. It gave me courage…to be honest, finally."

"I'm glad, too," he said as he brought her back into his arms. And this time he returned her kiss, showing her that this was not wasted time. This was time they'd both needed, a little respite before things turned ugly again. *Thank You, Lord,* she silently whispered, *for allowing me to see him as the man I love. And for showing me that he loves me, too.* That would be the test—if he still loved her when all of this was over.

For just a while, Selena was lost in that kiss, lost in what she'd known all along. She loved Brice. Loved him with a powerful force so strong that she felt light-headed just admitting it to herself. But how could she ever find the courage to admit it to him? That somehow scared her more than all the horrible things she'd found out about the people she'd trusted in her work—much more. But she couldn't give Brice her heart until those people were brought to justice and that meant she had to be honest with him. So she pulled back and stared up at him, seeing her own feelings there in his bright eyes. "Brice, I've found out some things on my own—"

A sound stopped her—a snap and a ping like a rock hitting glass. And then, she went down, down, pushed toward the floor as Brice covered her, then called out, screaming commands.

"Vern, get down. Bullet—it was a bullet! Vern, do you hear me?"

Someone had just tried to shoot at them.

And Vern wasn't responding to Brice's calls.

* * *

Brice pulled a gun out of the inside pocket of his tux, surprising Selena as he stood in front of her. "Stay behind the table," he ordered. "Don't leave this area."

She moved her head in acknowledgment, watching as he bent in a crouch and headed toward the spot where Vern had been posted. She shouldn't be shocked at seeing Brice with a sleek revolver, but her heart quickened at the implications of the weapon. Their romantic evening was as shattered now as the glass in the window.

"Vern, answer me," he called in a soft whisper.

"I'm here," came the weak reply. "Got it in the left shoulder, boss, but I'm good to go. Went in and out."

"Did you see anything?"

"Not a thing," Vern replied, his tone indicating that he'd failed in his job. "Whoever it was must have had a rifle with a night scope. Lucky for me, the bullet penetrated the glass door first and shifted a few inches. The open door protected me or I might be dead right now."

Selena swallowed the metallic taste of terror, willing herself to be strong. Now more than ever she needed to give Brice the information on the fake drugs. And now more than ever she wanted this over so she could just be with the man she loved. She hated cowering here under the table, but she didn't want to cause Brice or Vern to get hurt from having to save her.

"Selena?"

She heard Brice's sharp call. "Yes?"

"I'm checking on Vern. We can't get a response from the security guard posted outside. Stay down and don't move, okay?"

"All right."

The sounds that just minutes ago brought her joy now sent sinister shivers up her spine. The frogs calling, the birds cawing, the fountain splashing, all reminded her of her night alone and afraid hidden in the back of the village compound, waiting for Brice to come and find her. Waiting and clutching her bag with the pills she'd found. The fake pills that they'd been giving to patients.

Thank You, God, for sending him. If Brice hadn't come for her—she couldn't think past that. She was here now and she was alive. Her silent prayers lifted up like tiny birds, scattering and shifting into the heavens.

She raised her head, wondering what was going on. "Brice?"

"I'm here, luv. We're gonna get you out of here. Let's hope our guard is still nearby to help."

"I enjoyed our dinner," she said, tears forming in her eyes.

"Aye, me, too. Sorry I brought you to this glass-enclosed room, though. In hindsight, it probably wasn't such a good idea."

"No, no, it was wonderful. Just wonderful."

"Keep it quiet," Vern interjected. "They might still be out there."

Brice grunted. "That's why I'm going out to search around. Selena, Vern's coming to join you, okay? You can check his wound for me."

"Okay, but Brice, be careful."

"Always, luv." She heard the glass doors clicking shut.

The next thing Selena knew, Vern had crawled over

to sit beside her, his big eyes bright with pain, his smile shining with reassurance as she automatically began probing the bloody spot at the top of his left shoulder.

"Don't you worry none, sugah. Brice knows what he's doing. He'll get 'em."

Selena wanted to believe that, but right now her head filled with an image she couldn't shake. An image of Brice, lying wounded, or worse, dead.

And all because of her.

Brice hurried around the house, checking behind bushes and searching for signs of anyone lurking nearby. Because he'd checked the security system just before their meal, he was pretty sure the culprit wasn't on the premises but stationed somewhere in the nearby woods. But he had to look anyway just to be sure, and he really wished the security guard would respond on his radio. He scanned the bushes and trees, thinking the shooter could be long gone by now. The shooter obviously had been aiming for Selena.

She could have been killed right before his eyes tonight and all because he'd felt it necessary to push her into telling him the truth. Well, he'd learned a valuable lesson. Never again would he do that to her. From now on, things would be strictly business between them, no matter his need to know that she loved him, no matter his need to get to the bottom of what she was hiding. But…he reminded himself as he walked around the blossoming gardens, careful to look for shadows and movement, she had promised to reveal all. He'd get her back to her room and then they'd discuss what was going on and what to do next. And he'd keep things professional—which meant no more waltzing and kisses, even in a place he'd personally secured. No place was safe. He had to get a grip and get back to the job at hand.

Before it was too late.

Then he saw something shining in the bushes near the guardhouse just inside the front gate. His gun out, he crept to the spot and found the security guard, unconscious but still alive, his ID badge shimmering in the moonlight like a warning beacon.

Brice felt a huge bump on the man's head. The guard groaned, his eyes blinking open. "What happened?"

Brice filled him in as he helped the man sit up. "Are you okay?"

"I think so, sir. Just a bit fuzzy."

"What are you doing down here by the gate?"

"I heard a noise, a strange animal sound."

Brice let out a grunt. "So you came to investigate?"

"Yes, sir. Then…I think someone used a stun gun on me. I went down and I must have hit my head on a tree root. I blacked out until you came up."

"Can you walk?" Brice asked, carefully lifting the man to his feet.

The guard nodded his head. "They didn't get inside but I think they planned on trying. I heard a car crank up just before I got zapped. I guess they left."

"I'm sure they did," Brice replied. After checking the gate once again, he walked the man up to the house. "We'll get you some help." While he tried to figure out how to capture Selena's tormentors.

Selena appreciated the way Vern was trying to distract her with colorful stories of piloting airplanes and landing hot air balloons in the desert, but she wished he'd be quiet long enough for her to reexamine his injured shoulder. She applied direct pressure with her palm pressed tightly against a linen dinner napkin, then took a clean napkin and tied it tightly around the wound.

"The bullet went straight through as far as I can tell," she said, assured that he'd live at least. "I don't think anything is too severely damaged, but you still need to see a doctor to get that wound debrided and get you on some antibiotics."

"I'm fit as a fiddle, darlin'," the older man with the curly gray hair said, grinning. "I've been through worse, trust me. I've been shot and I've had bones broken in both arms and one of my legs. I'm tough."

"I believe you, but I don't want an infection to set in."

"I have a very strong immune system."

She could believe that, too, but focusing on his injury kept her mind off of Brice.

"I wonder what's taking that boy so long," Vern said, as if to echo her own concerns. "Maybe I'd better go check on him."

"Not without me," Selena said, getting up to crouch with him as he tried to move.

"True, I can't leave you here," Vern said. "The boss would have my hide for sure. I guess we'd better just sit tight."

Selena looked around for a weapon, then spotted the empty mineral-water bottle on the table. Grabbing the big sleek green bottle, she turned to Vern. "I can't just sit here. Let's go find him."

"Let me try with the radio first," Vern said, speaking

in a strong whisper into his tiny walkie-talkie phone. "Brice, come in."

"Are you still alive and armed?" came the reply.

Vern chuckled. "I've still got my pistol."

"Get her to the interior of the house then."

"Will do." He helped Selena up, telling her to stay in a crouch. "Brice wants us to get on the move."

Selena was more than ready. She held up the bottle in one hand and her cell phone in the other, just in case she had to call for help. "Good. You can shoot anyone who messes with us, then I'll finish the job with a good whack to the head."

"You are your father's daughter."

"You can say that again," she retorted. She was tired of cowering in corners. This had to stop. If she wanted a life with Brice, she had to end this tonight.

They slinked through the door into the formal dining room, staying close to walls while Vern worked to secure the room.

"Let's get away from the windows," Vern whispered, winded but still walking, his gun poised in his right hand. He stayed in front of her, holding his injured left arm back behind him so he could keep her close. "Brice will meet us inside."

Selena felt her cell phone vibrating against her palm. Seeing the number, she said, "It's Dr. Jarrell. He only calls me if it's an emergency."

"Do you have to answer it now?" Vern asked.

"I'll make it quick," she said, too frightened to let it keep vibrating. "Hello?"

"Selena, I've found the culprit. I think I've tracked the source of the counterfeit drugs. It's over."

"I hope so," Selena said. "We just got shot at."

"Oh, no." There was a pause, then the doctor's next words shocked her. "Selena, I think I'm in trouble. I got in a fight with Greg Gordon. I found out he's the one behind all of this. And now…he's dead."

"Dead?" Shocked, Selena slumped against the dark wall while Vern kept watch. "What happened?"

"The boy was up to his eyeballs in this. He was in cahoots with our on-site pharmacist and an online distributor and he admitted the Night Walkers were smuggling counterfeit drugs in and out of our clinic in Día Belo while he handled things here. We argued and he pulled a gun and, well, we struggled and it went off. He's not responding."

"Where are you?"

"At the clinic, in my office. I need help, Selena."

"Did you call the police?"

"No, not yet. I need you and Brice to come and tell me what to do. Please?"

Selena stood silent, then glanced over at Vern. He raised his gun as they heard footsteps.

"Vern, it's me," Brice called out. "I have the other guard with me."

Vern lowered the gun as Brice hurried up the hallway, his gaze centered on Selena. Vern helped him settle the guard down in a chair. "Who is she talking to?" he asked Vern.

Vern shrugged. "It don't sound good, whoever it is."

"I'll be there as soon as I can, Dr. Jarrell."

Selena hung up the phone and explained what the doctor had told her. "Dr. Jarrell's in trouble. He had a confrontation with Greg Gordon and, somehow, Greg was shot. He said Greg was behind all of the threats—because of a counterfeit drug ring."

Brice's gaze slammed with hers. That matched what Shane had said—"Watch the intern." Brice couldn't believe Selena would have tried to protect Greg. "Is that what you wanted to tell me?"

She hesitated, then said, "I didn't…I had no idea about Greg. I have to go to the clinic. Dr. Jarrell is there and Greg is dead. Please, Brice, can you take me there…so we can call the police?"

Someone had just tried to shoot her and still she wouldn't tell him the truth. "It might not be safe."

"I have to go," she said. "If Greg is dead, then this is over, finally. I need to be there with Dr. Jarrell."

Brice frowned, then pushed a hand through his hair. Had Greg been working with the Night Walkers? Had he hired one of them to terrorize Selena? He needed to talk to Dr. Jarrell. "Aye, and we'll have to give the police a full statement." His eyes held hers, a scattered disbelief moving through his gaze. "And on the way you can explain exactly what you've been keeping from me." He grabbed her by the arm. "And why you felt it necessary to withhold information." He glanced at Vern's injury. "Do you need medical attention?"

Vern shook his head. "I'm fine for now. I'll clean it up and doctor it myself."

The guard told Brice he was okay, too. They agreed to stay put and watch the house until they heard from Brice.

Satisfied with that, Brice pulled Selena through the house and out into the garage until they'd reached the

Jaguar, his mind racing. If Gregory Gordon was behind all of this, then that explained why he'd taken Selena out on that boat. And it also showed how desperate the man had become.

Brice didn't speak as he helped her in and settled behind the wheel. Selena shook with fear and dread as she tried to find the words to explain everything. "Brice, I think I was wrong. I thought…I thought Diego was involved."

Brice drove the Jag with expert precision around the curve in the driveway leading away from the house. "Start from the beginning," he said as they reached the tall gates. He hit a button, tapping his fingers impatiently as they waited.

Holding on, Selena braced herself for the ride to the clinic. "I should have told you, but I was so confused. They took our drugs, but it's not what you think."

He shifted gears, sending the car into a purr of efficiency. "I'm all ears now, luv." About a mile from the gate, Brice made a left onto a deserted two-lane highway with high bluffs on each side.

"This isn't easy," she said, swallowing back dread.

"Selena, just tell me," he said, his tone impatient and full of frustration. "Tell me now, before the police get involved. It's the only way I can help you."

Selena looked up as headlights approached. Then she heard a pop and the car shuddered as Brice hit the brakes. The windshield shattered into a million shards of hanging glass, the car spinning out of control.

Brice gripped the steering wheel as the car skidded toward the nearby hills and bluffs. Another shot rang out, hitting the hood. The third shot blew out a tire. He pushed her down, then knuckled the spinning steering wheel. "Hold on and stay down!"

FOURTEEN

Selena held her head down, her breath trapped in a scream as Brice spun the car around toward the encroaching bluffs. "We have to get you out of this car!"

But it was too late. A big dark sedan skidded toward them, then slammed to a halt against the Jag's front fender, blocking the road as it pushed the Jag up against the brush and trees. They were trapped near a hilly dropoff.

Brice hissed a breath as he reached for his gun, the sound of crickets singing all around them. "Sit tight."

Selena glanced up to see two figures approaching their car. A tall man stepped out of the shadows, a bittersweet smile on his face. Holding a pistol toward them, he said, "It's just me, dear."

"Dr. Jarrell?" Then Selena turned sick to her stomach. *He* was in on the counterfeit drug operation? And she'd told him everything. Him, instead of Brice. All of her hopes vanished into the night as a solid dread gripped her heart.

"I'm so sorry," he called as he motioned for the other man standing behind him. "Would you both kindly get out of the car? And Brice, hand your weapon to my friend here, please, so I don't have to use this gun."

Brice nodded to her. "It's going to be all right."

They got out of the car and came around to face Dr. Jarrell. A cool, earthy-smelling breeze mixed with the smell of burned tire rubber as it rustled around the moon-dappled woods. Somewhere, an owl hooted. Brice held his gun out, barrel down, toward the man in the shadows.

"Put it on the asphalt and slide it across to him," Dr. Jarrell ordered.

Brice lowered the gun to the road and shoved it forward, but when the man stepped into the light, Selena gasped. "Greg?"

Brice remained silent, his eyes centered on the two men. Selena searched his face and through the moon's glow, saw a pulse jumping in his jaw.

Greg Gordon, the man who'd taken her out on the boat on Lake Lanier, the man who was supposed to be dead now, gave her a pleading, nervous nod as he bent to pick up the gun. He was very much alive.

And suddenly, Selena remembered the voice that had threatened her over the phone. "You've both been in on this, haven't you?"

The doctor's dark smile held a sinister sneer. "You remember my young friend?"

Selena lifted her chin toward Greg. "Of course I do. Did you plan that little boat trip just to silence me—after the bomb scare didn't work?"

Dr. Jarrell nodded. "I had no choice, dear. I couldn't be sure what you had seen or heard. I was hoping Greg might make this easier for me but he didn't get very far.

First he messes up the bomb, then he panics out on the boat. He was supposed to *pretend* to be drunk, but he got nervous and overindulged on his meds and alcohol—to the point of being incompetent. He's addicted to painkillers and booze, I'm afraid."

Selena's stomach roiled with the realization of that night. "Brice got there before Greg succeeded."

The doctor waved his gun, his head bobbing. "It was supposed to be a tragic accident. A drowning."

Brice took a step, but the doctor lifted the sleek pistol toward Selena. "We're just talking here, Whelan, so don't be a hero."

Brice shook his head, but he stepped back, putting his body between Selena and the gun. "Oh, I'm no hero. Not a'tall. But I will do what I have to do to keep you from making a big mistake." He glanced at Greg. "Or should I say *another* big mistake."

Greg squirmed and squinted, his rifle shaking. "I didn't want to do it. I couldn't drown you and I didn't want to shoot at you tonight. I just thought I'd scare you."

"I'm a very good swimmer," Selena countered, gaining strength as her rage took over. "And I don't scare that easily." It wasn't true, but she needed a courageous front right now. "By the way, your aim is way off."

Brice shot her a warning glance but Selena didn't care. She'd had enough. She turned on the doctor. "So you were behind everything? And you lured me out from the protection of Brice's estate tonight to end all of this?"

The doctor nodded. "The Night Walkers aren't after you, Selena. They raided the village over a discrepancy—so we were forced to shut down the clinic. When you…survived and came home, we didn't know if you'd found out our little secret so we'd hoped the bomb would be enough. But…I should have known you'd not give in easily. So after I found out you were under Brice's protection, I had Greg make the signal calls and I gave him your cell number—both just warnings to scare you. I taught him the signal sound myself, after hearing it down in the jungle. It was the signal the Night Walkers gave when they were ready to move another shipment." He shrugged. "And when I wasn't at the Día Belo clinic, another clinic worker took over. He was a member of the Night Walkers."

Selena let out a held breath. "Did you set up the hit on the clinic?"

"No," the doctor replied. "Things got too complicated. Your friend Diego had suspicions after several villagers became ill. The Night Walkers decided to take matters into their own hands. They didn't trust anyone, so no one was suppose to survive, not even their inside man."

"But Selena did survive," Brice said, disgust evident in his tone. "So you had to come after her, but you also had to be very careful that no one suspected you."

"I told you, I didn't have any choice since she wouldn't talk much about what she'd seen down there. I knew it was just a matter of time though, before she figured things out."

"And how exactly did you ship the drugs?" Brice asked, his words as calm as the whispering wind, his gaze sliding over Selena. His look told her he wondered how she'd found out. And she was sure he'd get to that question soon, too.

"We stuffed some of the medicine inside the toys when necessary. Most of the time we just shipped drugs openly from the distribution center right here in Atlanta to both the clinics. The packaging is so good, it's hard to distinguish which is real and which isn't. The rest of the drugs were shipped from a location in China. We had several diversions set up—secondary wholesalers, repacking, and an iron-clad system of online ordering. It was foolproof." He glared at Greg. "Or at least it should have been."

"And Greg helped you with this?" Selena asked, her blood pressure rising until she became dizzy.

"Greg is a *very weak* accomplice, but yes, he wanted to learn at my feet, so to speak. But he got a bit too addicted and a bit too greedy with the Night Walkers and made a lot of noise about wanting more of the cut. Your friend Diego figured things out and inadvertently discussed it with the pharmacist who reported back to the Night Walkers, so they retaliated by destroying our clinic." The doctor looked over at Greg. "A huge setback on Greg's account. But he's here tonight to redeem himself."

Selena pointed in the air toward Greg. "So Diego had to die, but *he* gets to live?"

"Only because he's blackmailing me," Greg said on an angry wail. "I'll lose everything if the truth comes out." He lifted his gun. "Let's just get this over with."

"Good idea." Dr. Jarrell motioned to Greg. "Kill the man and put him in the car. I only want Selena."

Greg looked panicked. "You told me no more killing. You said you just wanted to talk to her."

"Do you want to go to jail for a long, long time?"

Greg wiped at his face, then walked toward Brice. "I'm sorry." He held up the rifle, but he didn't fire. His hands were shaking too hard.

Brice glanced over at Selena, his eyes locking with hers. "Whatever happens, don't leave here with these two, you hear me? You fight, Selena. You fight."

Selena bobbed her head while Dr. Jarrell rushed toward them. "She's going with us, all right. But you're not going to live to see it. Unlike my spineless friend here, I'm a very good shot."

Impatient, he turned his own gun toward Brice but Selena rushed in front of Brice. "I'll go. I'll do whatever you want. Just don't kill him, please."

Brice stared in horror at the scene being played out on the dark road. Did Selena think for one minute he'd let her get in that car with this psycho? Of course, if he got shot then she'd really be in trouble. So he had to stay alive. And he had to keep his wits. The doctor had just confessed to them, so he obviously didn't plan on letting any of them live. Including Greg.

"What do you plan to do?" he asked, stalling for time and praying Vern would get tired of waiting to hear from him.

Dr. Jarrell kept his gun steady. "I need to explain, Selena. This is all a big misunderstanding. If we can work together to make it right—"

"You just admitted everything," Selena said. "You can't make this right! You killed innocent people and for what? More money? Why? To keep the clinics running or to keep your lavish lifestyle on track? How can you explain that?"

Brice watched the doctor's scowling face, then

glanced over at Greg. The younger man was shaking and obviously scared—and probably high. Brice decided to take full advantage of that.

"Greg, it's not too late to *really* redeem yourself. You can testify against this man and probably get a much lighter sentence. Think about it—felony, trafficking in unapproved drugs, wire and mail fraud, and engaging in a criminal enterprise—that's gonna be one tough sentence, unless you give up the goods."

Greg's eyes widened with doubt. "No way am I falling for that promise. I'm in this too deep. I was in from the first when he offered me the world on a platter, right alone with a bottle of pills to ease my stress. I wanted to impress him so much, I fell for it!"

"You never complained," Dr. Jarrell shouted over his shoulder. "You just got greedy and went behind my back, making deals with the Night Walkers even after I warned you about how dangerous they were. It's your fault we're standing here tonight."

Brice shot a gaze toward Selena. "That's a heavy accusation, Greg. Are you going to take the fall for an operation he's clearly masterminded?"

Greg looked unsure, then turned defiant. "I don't want to. I didn't want to strap that bomb to Selena's car and I sure didn't want to throw her in the lake. He made me call her and scare her and he made me sneak inside that creepy compound of yours right after you left for the lake. I had to hurry to make it back to the party."

Brice calculated the timetable in his mind. It was doable. "You mean, when my young associate was working on the security system, right?"

Greg shrugged. "A lucky break. I just happened to

be in the right place at the right time. I waited until the old ladies left and managed to get through the gate without the cameras seeing me."

"Because Roderick had taken the system down."

"Whatever, man. I got in, did my thing and got out. I don't like that place."

Brice thought Greg did have some sense, after all. "I don't blame you. You committed several crimes on my property. No fond memories for you, but something I surely won't forget."

"I wish I could forget all of this."

"Shut up," Dr. Jarrell shouted, taking Greg's gun out of his shaking hand. Tossing the rifle behind him, he held up the pistol. "I'm sick of your constant whining, Gordon. You think you'll ever be a good doctor, well, you're wrong. Dead wrong if you can't do what I tell you." He whirled toward Greg, the gun bobbing.

Brice moved in a flash, grabbing Selena to shove her out of the way. "Run!"

"Brice!" she shouted as she fell into the shadows.

Brice lunged toward the doctor, trying to grab at the gun. Dr. Jarrell jerked away, struggling as he frantically turned the gun on Brice. Brice shook him off, pushing at the gun's barrel, grunting as he tripped against the doctor. He fell just as the shot rang out.

Selena screamed somewhere in the nearby trees.

The bullet meant for Brice hit Greg in the chest and he fell to the ground, blood spilling from his wound. Brice scrambled to retrieve his own gun, then flipped onto his back and saw Selena running toward him.

"Selena, no!"

Brice watched in horror as the doctor lunged toward

Selena and caught her, shoving her in front of him, the gun pointed toward her ribs.

Brice called out, his heart rigid with dread, his gun steady even if his heartbeat wasn't. Staying on his back with his hands holding the gun and his head up, he said, "Let her go. Now."

Dr. Jarrell whirled so he could see Brice. "You need to put that gun away and get up, Whelan."

Brice tried another tactic but he didn't drop his gun. And he stayed on the ground. "We can talk this out. Just let her go."

The doctor shook his head. "Like I said, she's going with me, one way or another. If you try to stop me, she'll die right here."

"I can't let you leave with her," Brice countered, his gun still leveled on the doctor's forehead. "I can shoot you from here." If he kept his cool.

"Not if I shoot her first," the doctor called out. "Drop the gun, Whelan." He pressed his weapon against Selena's flesh. "I'm a good shot, too, remember. I had to learn how to protect myself."

"So he could traffic in counterfeit drugs," Selena called out. "He won't stop until he kills us. Don't listen to him, Brice."

"She's right, and her bravado is impressive," the doctor said. "But not only am I a good shot, I also know exactly where to put the bullet to kill her instantly. What's it gonna be? Now get up and give me the gun."

Brice met Selena's steady gaze. She wasn't afraid. But he sure was. He couldn't take a chance on watching her die and he refused to let this man take her with him. He'd never see her again. So he finally lowered his gun to the ground, careful to keep his eyes on the man holding Selena. Then he stood, both hands out, and used the last weapon he had left—his pride. "I'd like to hear how Selena figured things out. *Without me.*"

Selena twisted her head to glare up at the doctor, then turned back to Brice, her chin up, her eyes defiant. "I first suspected after the Night Walkers came through. I found some odd colored pills scattered on the floor. They didn't match any of the medications we had on-site."

"She's too clever," Dr. Jarrell said. "Such a shame."

He stepped farther away, toward the open car door, pulling her along with him. "Now, dear girl, tell him how you went out *on your own* to find the proof." He pushed the gun deep into the satin of her dress. "You failed to mention that to your guardian, didn't you?"

Selena didn't answer, but she gave Brice a guilty, pleading look. She *did* have proof. And she *had* found it without telling him. At last he knew what she'd been hiding. And that certainly had to be what she'd planned on telling him tonight. Admitting that now, however, put her in even more danger. This man would kill her to keep her quiet. *Dear God,* he prayed, *what has she done? How can I save her now? Help me, Lord.*

"Talk to me, Selena," he said. "What else did you discover?" It was a long shot, but if he could stall Dr. Jarrell, he might be able to save her.

"She isn't going to talk to anyone except me," Dr. Jarrell said, his voice shrill and echoing. "Poor girl, she's so confused and so very paranoid. She's going with me so I can explain things to her. Then everything will be fine, back the way it was before. We'll be safe and away from everyone."

Brice's gut instincts kicked in. The man was going to take her out of the country. And what he'd do to her once they got there, Brice didn't want to think. Not good. Not good at all.

Selena moved her head slightly. "I'll be all right, Brice. Dr. Jarrell doesn't really want to kill me. He must have a very good reason for doing this, but I believe he's too honorable for murder." She glanced down to where Greg lay so silent and still, her expression in direct opposition to her words.

Brice was awed by her negotiation tactics. And her courage. But he knew if this man took her, she'd most likely be dead before morning.

"We can discuss it right here," he said, his gaze shifting from the doctor to Selena. "I'm a good listener and I can negotiate you a deal. You can go free, Doc. Just tell me what you want."

Dr. Jarrell snorted a response. "I'll just reckon you are a good listener, but no deal. You're being paid an extravagant salary for guarding her but you haven't done a very good job, have you? She didn't even trust you enough to tell you anything. My friend Delton isn't going to be happy. But he won't be back in time to save her. And no one will come for her—not where I'm taking her. Her death will be on your head."

"No, sir," Brice retorted, his tone clear and precise in spite of the rapid pulse hitting his temple. "Her death will always be on your head. And I will hunt you down until you pay, trust me. So I suggest you take me up on my offer."

"You can come after me, but I'll be long gone," the doctor said on a winded breath. "I've made arrangements to disappear so I don't need you. You can't save the day this time, Whelan."

Brice wanted to shout at the man that *he* would save Selena, but Dr. Jarrell was right on one account. Brice had failed in protecting her and now she might die because of him. He should have forced the truth out of her from the beginning.

"I'm sure we can work something out," he said, trying again. "You're a renowned physician, a pillar of the community. People will stand by you. Just explain things to us, here and now, how and why you're involved in something illegal. We'll help you."

Selena nodded, following Brice's lead. "I'm willing to help you, Dr. Jarrell. Think of Liz and your children—your grandchildren."

"Shut up," the doctor shouted, his tone shrill and frantic. "We're leaving now, Selena. And if you try to fight me, I'll kill him—I'll kill both of you and get it over with. I have too much at stake to give up now." He looked at Brice, hatred in his eyes. "And I'd be glad to get him out of my sight, once and for all."

He started backing toward the open car door, keeping Selena in front of him as a shield. Brice thought about his options. His cell was in the car but sending out an alarm could prove too much danger for Selena—she still might get shot. If he tried to make a move toward the doctor, things could go from bad to worse.

He was trapped—another stupid mistake.

But he intended to make up for all his mistakes, if he had to die trying. Because he didn't intend to let Selena leave with this crazy doctor. Even if it meant exposing CHAIM to the world at large.

"I'm taking her," the doctor said, determination grating through his words. "If you move, I will shoot her here and now."

Brice tried once again. "It's not too late, sir. We can do this without involving the authorities."

Dr. Jarrell's expression shifted between remorse and resolve. "No, I can't talk to you. If I have her with me, it'll give me more time. I just need more time." He raised the gun, pushing it hard against Selena's side. "I need her so you won't come after me." He pushed Selena toward the driver's side of the sedan. "Enough! Open the door and get in. You're driving."

Brice tried to find his next breath. The man had said he was going to silence her forever and he'd tried with threats, a bomb attack and a bullet through the solarium glass tonight. He needed to *eliminate* her. Brice could dive for his gun, roll and aim, hoping to hit the doctor. But Selena could get caught in the cross fire. Or he could let them go, follow them and try to get Selena away from this sicko.

She must have read his mind. "Brice, I'll be okay." Her smile was shaky, but her eyes held a definite message. "Remember the cotillion and that football player?"

Brice tried to focus. He remembered the guy had gotten into Selena's car and then refused to get out. She'd somehow convinced the drunk teen that if he'd take her back inside the country club she'd dance with him the rest of the night. But after he'd opened the car door, Selena had gunned the gas and left the boy spinning in the wind. And Brice had taken over from there—once he'd found the idiot.

"I remember, luv," he said, terrified to let her go. But was she telling him to do just that because she had a plan? "That was such a night, wasn't it?"

"Yes. Just remember that. I can take care of myself."

She gave Brice one more open-eyed glance. "You have to…let me go, Brice. You have to trust me."

She wanted him to trust her? *Now?* Not now, when his heart was screaming, when sweat was popping out along his spine. Not now, when he wanted her back in his arms dancing to beautiful music, no matter how mad he was at her for not leveling with him. He watched as Dr. Jarrell backed Selena toward the car, then he gave her a long look, hoping she could see into his heart. "Don't worry, luv. I'll be right here."

Selena smiled, nodding her head, tears trailing down her face. "I know you will. You've always been right there."

"Shut up and start the car," the doctor shouted. He glared at Brice. "Don't move until we're out of sight. Your car is useless now, but if you send anyone after us, I'll end it all right here."

All Brice could do was watch, coming unglued piece by piece as he stood holding his breath. Only for Selena's sake, he told himself. Only for Selena. He decided to trust her as she'd asked him to do, and he prayed to God, putting his trust in a higher power, too.

While Brice's prayer had been well placed, the doctor had miscalculated his head nurse. Just as Dr. Jarrell opened the door and leaned down to get inside, Selena cranked the vehicle and hit the gas. The open door knocked the doctor down and back. He fell to the ground next to the still body of Greg Gordon. And

Brice, shocked and amazed, didn't waste any time pouncing onto the groaning doctor. He lifted the man up. "You were right. She is very clever."

Dr. Jarrell rolled his eyes, groaned and then passed out.

Selena stopped the car a few feet away then got out, her hand holding the door to steady her. "Can we get out of here now?"

Brice let the doctor fall back to the ground then ran to pull her into his arms. "Not before I make sure you're all right," he said, dragging his hands through her hair.

"I'm fine now." She held to him, her body trembling. "Brice, I—"

He saw so much there in her eyes. Pain. Despair. Hope. Guilt. And love.

He kissed her just to keep from having to deal with all of that. Except the love. He's seen her love for him in her eyes and now he felt it in her sweet, demanding kiss.

Knowing that held him together. For now.

"Let's call for help," he said as he tugged her toward his car. "Then we'll get out of here."

Later, when he'd had time to think about it, it would sink in that she had once again kept him at arm's length. She hadn't trusted him enough to give him the missing key to this whole puzzle—the key that would have unlocked this case and saved both of them a lot of angst. And this time it had almost cost her life.

FIFTEEN

"This, my friend, is a messy business."

Brice had to agree with Sir Shane Warwick. "The messiest."

Shane took a sip of his Earl Grey tea, his crystal blue eyes assessing Brice with just enough scrutiny to make Brice wince. "Let me see if I have all the details," he said, his British accent low and clear. "You're in love with Selena Carter and you've always been in love with Selena Carter. Yet you agreed to be her bodyguard while you also agreed to track down the henchmen who raided the village of Día Belo on the Argentina/Brazil border and left everyone except Selena for dead? And all of that aside, your research and investigation told you right up front that Selena was hiding something, yet you—being an expert in interrogation tactics—never thought to sit the woman down and force her to give up the goods? And now, we have a messy cleanup involving a prominent Atlanta physician, a dead intern who, according to Dr. Jarrell, was the one making strange cat calls around your property and threatening phone calls to Selena— not to mention a bad attempt at a bomb and a botched attempt to drown Selena. And we find that a CHAIM-funded missionary operation has been dealing in the underground economy by producing and pushing counterfeit drugs on the international market? How am I doing so far, old boy?"

Brice really hated Warwick's way of summing things up with deliberate, accurate calculations. "That pretty much covers everything, yes."

Shane straightened the high-backed kitchen chair he'd been tilting on two legs. "May I just ask—what in the world were you thinking?"

Brice had asked himself that very question over and over throughout this long night. Now that he'd had time to go back over the facts, he could see it all so clearly. Too little, too late. He'd botched things from the get-go. But at least Dr. Jarrell would be brought to justice.

Running a hand down his beard shadow, he shook his head. "I guess I was thinking I had to protect the woman I love, no matter the consequences."

Shane made a tsk-tsk noise. "I see. Been there myself at times. Very gallant of you. But did it ever occur to you that you were way too close to this situation to be objective and clearheaded?"

Brice got up to toss his coffee dregs in the sink. It was near dawn and they were alone in the kitchen, the eerie quiet of early morning surrounding them while everyone else was still asleep. "Why, yes, Shane, that did occur to me last night when I watched that crazy doctor holding a gun on Selena."

"A little late, that, but good that it came to you all the same. And no harm done. We have the good doctor at an undisclosed location, spilling the beans to the proper CHAIM authorities, and Selena is sound asleep upstairs—we hope." His dark eyebrows lifted. "Now, to get all the nasty details done away with so we can turn this over to…oh, maybe the CIA, FDA, FBI, SIS, Interpol and whatever other world authority that might be interested."

Brice stared at the coming dawn, his doubt and disgust rising up inside him just as that brilliant morning sun was rising up through the trees, hot and full of fury. "I blew it, okay. I know that. But I was getting nowhere on any of this. Dr. Jarrell's background check came back clean and from what you've told me, we only had Gordon's very secretive drug addiction—nothing concrete to tie him to any of this. But I can't make excuses. I shouldn't have taken her word that she didn't know anything and I shouldn't have exposed her when I planned a romantic dinner out in the solarium. No, make that, I should have never brought her *into* this house. Her presence totally clouded my vision and judgment."

Shane grunted in agreement. "I can understand your need to woo her into confessing. I mean, she's a very pretty woman and I'm all for mixing a little business with pleasure, but—"

"But I wasn't thinking clearly," Brice finished. "I know that now. I know what could have happened last night." He'd relived each moment over and over throughout the long night.

Shane got up to come and stand beside him, looking unwrinkled and unruffled in his tailor-made suit in spite of his long flight across the Atlantic and his even longer night making sure the doctor had been taken into custody and Greg Gordon's body had been taken to the coroner. "And yet, she's here with you and she's safe and we're getting somewhere on this case now—in fact, I'd say it's just about a wrap. Not bad for a night's work."

"It could have gone the other way," Brice said in a low growl.

Shane slapped a hand on his arm. "But it didn't. So we go from here and make things right."

"Her father will be back tomorrow and he's expecting a full report," Brice said. "And as for me—I'll probably be sent back to Ireland on the first ship leaving the dock. I never dreamed I'd be one to have to go into isolation at my own retreat."

"Ah, but you love that place," Shane said with a wry grin. "And…it is almost shearing season, now, isn't it?"

"You're making me feel much better," Brice countered. Then he glanced toward the kitchen stairs. "I guess I need to…finish this job. I need to talk to Selena."

"That would be the first course of business," Shane replied. "And meantime, I'll put together a preliminary report on what we've found so far, based on Dr. Jarrell's statement and the information I managed to gather before I arrived."

"The doctor's background was clean," Brice said again. He'd hidden his secret life completely, but Warwick had found out a lot about the doctor since last night. He enjoyed living in luxury and he'd funded the good life by selling cheap counterfeit drugs at marked-up prices to unsuspecting health care facilities and pharmacies. And just to fuel his fun he'd skimmed off the top, trying to save money at his own clinics.

"I can't believe the man had such little regard for the people he was supposed to be serving," Shane said, shaking his head. "His words to me were that they were poor and expendable, destined to die early anyway. To which I replied he was despicable."

"He is a monster," Brice replied. "I think he even had Selena brainwashed into protecting him."

"She'll need time to heal, Brice."

Brice nodded. "I guess I'd better get on with it."

"Let me know what happens," Shane said, his tone sympathetic.

"We'll compare notes later then," Brice said, turning toward the stairs. He stopped at the steps. "And Warwick, I'm glad you're here."

Shane pivoted on his expensive, custom-made shoes. "Think nothing of it, old boy. I owe you one…or two."

"That you do," Brice said, smiling for the first time since last night.

But when he got to the door of Selena's room, he stopped smiling. He was about to ambush the woman he loved because he had to get information for his job. It wouldn't be easy but then Selena hadn't made this easy. This conversation would either make them or break them. But it had to be done. He'd held off the local authorities too long already. But before they questioned her, Brice had to do the same. For his own peace of mind.

He was about to knock when his mother came walking down the hallway, still in her robe and slippers, her silver-blond hair pulled up in a dainty top-knot. "Hello, darling," she said, her hand automatically reaching up to touch his jaw. "Tough night?"

"The worst."

"And you can't talk about it, of course."

"No, not yet. Maybe not ever."

Adele gave him a reassuring look. "I'll send up hot tea, coffee and some muffins."

"Thank you, Mum." Brice kissed her. "We'll be in my office. Go get your own breakfast, too. Shane's down in the kitchen."

"Ah, Sir Shane Warwick. Such a lovely man."

"Don't let him chat you up too much."

Adele lifted her arched eyebrows. "Oh, I don't mind Shane's flirting. He's an adorable man."

Brice chuckled at that. Shane did have a way with women of all ages. Maybe he should let Shane talk to Selena. But no, that had been Brice's job and he'd purposely failed. But not now. Not this morning.

So he knocked on the door and prepared himself for this interrogation. And prayed to the Lord he wasn't the one who caved first.

Selena was awake; she'd been expecting this knock. After all, Brice hadn't said more than a few words on the way home last night. He'd probably been too busy putting together all the pieces of her deception to talk. And she'd been too shocked to speak. Shocked and afraid of what she'd lost.

No, that wasn't exactly true. She'd tried the minute they'd gotten into the car with Roderick. "Brice, I'm sorry."

"You're tired and upset," he'd said. "And we need to be clear on the details when we take you in for your statement. Tomorrow, luv. First thing tomorrow morning. Then you can explain. Plenty of time for that now that we have the doctor in custody."

But now…*her* time was up. She knew what he wanted this morning. He wanted the truth, with no frills and no pretty words. She hoped she'd have the courage to give him that truth. And that he'd have the compassion to forgive her.

So she took a deep breath, checked her long blue sweater and matching blue knit pants and opened the door with a strained smile. "Brice, come in."

He shook his head. "I need you to come with me."

Selena didn't like the brisk tone, nor the way he avoided eye contact with her. If he'd just look at her the way he'd looked at her while they'd danced last night.

She shuddered, remembering Dr. Jarrell's gun hitting against her rib cage, remembering the solid wall of terror that had held her back, afraid the doctor would kill Brice if she didn't cooperate with him. She'd tried to help matters, tried to salvage the situation by taking things into her own hands. But in the process, she'd broken that fragile trust Brice had so needed to see.

And now, it was payback time.

He opened the heavy double doors of his private study at the back of the house, then motioned toward a deep leather chair centered in front of a wall-to-wall bookcase. "Sit here."

Selena sank down, her heart tapping a warning as she watched him tug at the wide wooden blinds lining the wall behind his massive desk. Morning sunshine rushed through the dark, masculine room as if attempting to shine a glaring spotlight right on Selena. She squinted and dropped deeper into her chair.

"Mother is bringing up breakfast for you."

"I'm not very hungry."

"You need to eat. And I know how you like your morning coffee."

"I could use a cup of that, yes." For fortitude, for that courage she was always grasping to find. "Brice—"

"Let's wait…until after Mum leaves."

She understood now. He was going to punish her. He was going into interrogator mode—to block the pain she'd inflicted inside his heart. Why, oh why, hadn't she just trusted him, asked for his help, saved him all this misery and confusion? *Why, dear Lord, am I so very stubborn and determined to do things my way? Help me now, give me humility, take away the pride that's held me back.*

The silence was stilted and telling, the sun's rays glaring and unforgiving. The seconds ticked away, the old pendulum clock on the wall swinging back and forth as a constant reminder of what she'd had and lost in one beautiful, tragic night. She was to the point of coming out of her skin when she heard footsteps and looked up to find Adele's sympathetic eyes on her.

"I'll only be a minute," Adele said. "I brought fresh bread and some cranberry muffins. Shane suggested a strong breakfast tea, but I told him you prefer coffee. I brought both."

Adele seemed as skittish as Selena felt. She stood to help with the tray but Adele shook her head. "Stay there, Selena. I've got it."

Even Brice's sweet mother seemed curt this morning.

Thankful and fearful after Adele discreetly shut the door and left, Selena heard the toll of doom in the clicking of the lock. Yes, her time was up and she had no one to blame but herself.

He turned, fully prepared to get down to business but when his gaze clashed with hers, any thoughts of professional cruelty and curtness left his brain. Goodness, why did she look so lovely sitting there in blue with the morning sun changing her hair from bronze to amber to gold with each shift of its rays?

He poured coffee and pushed a delicate flower-edged china cup full of the steaming brew toward her. "Drink."

She took a tentative sip.

He put a muffin on a matching plate. "Eat."

Selena stared at the muffin, then pushed the plate back toward him. "Is this how you talk to people who are forced to come and visit you at the castle?"

He pushed a hand through his hair. "It *is* my job."

"And I'm sure you're very good at it. Good at fixing CHAIM agents who go astray, good at breaking criminals before CHAIM turns them and all the evidence over to the proper authorities." She leaned forward, her eyes devoid of fear or reprisal. "But are you good at forgiveness, Brice? Because that's what I really need right now."

He braced himself against that soft, feminine plea. "I can forgive, luv. I've forgiven lots of times and asked for forgiveness myself at times. But, my darlin' Selena, I have a very hard time forgetting." He swallowed and held a hand on the back of his neck. "For example, I can't forget the way my heart went from dancing on cloud nine to the pits of despair last night. When I saw… when I saw him holding that gun on you, I saw nothing but a bleak future. A future without you. If I'd lost you—"

She was up, facing him across the desk. "But you didn't lose me, Brice. You didn't. I should have told you about the pills I found on the clinic floor, yes. I should have told you about the strange noises in your yard—that I recognized them that first night and knew they were meant for me. I should have told you about the cell phone call right after it happened. And yes, I should have told you the one thing I couldn't admit to myself. I suspected Dr. Jarrell, the man I admired and worked with and considered a second father, but I didn't tell you any of that. I couldn't. I didn't want to face that truth. I didn't want to face what it all meant—it was just too much. So I tried to fix this on my own and I messed up and I'm sorry. But I'm here now. And I'm telling you that you didn't lose me last night. You didn't. Brice, please."

He looked away from her tears.

Then his fist came down so hard on the old desk, coffee splashed from her cup, causing her to flinch. "I didn't *lose* you, Selena, because I never *had* you. All these years, we've turned to each other for so many things and the one time you needed me the most, I was at a loss because I knew you weren't being honest with me. Why? I can't for the life of me fathom why you couldn't trust me enough to *let me help you.* Can you answer me that one question, luv? Can you? Or are you as involved as the good doctor?"

To her credit, she didn't back down. She just stood there with her hands fisted against the wood, staring across at him with those luminous violet-blue eyes. Then she lowered her gaze and let out a sigh. "I was afraid, Brice, but I was not involved. At least not until

I got suspicious. I found those pills and I thought they'd robbed us to *get* to the drugs. They took drugs, yes, and they trashed the place and spilled out pills on the floor. That made me wonder what they wanted. Then I thought maybe they came at us to get even because…I thought maybe Diego was involved. But now I know *he* confronted the Night Walkers. And I've wished a hundred times over that I'd listened to him in the days before the attack. He'd made a few comments about patients getting sick even after being given medicine, but he never told me his suspicions. After the attack, I couldn't prove anything, so I just held my concerns, praying that I was wrong. But I sent the pills off to be analyzed. And then, Mr. Cooper died and I knew something wasn't right there either. I sent some of his Digoxin to the toxicology lab, too."

"So you went behind my back and had his drugs analyzed?"

"Yes, those and some of the pills I found at the clinic, just as I've said," she replied, nodding. "I had to know for myself before I could go to Dr. Jarrell. But I told him the minute I got the lab reports back. And he promised me he'd call in the FDA and issue an immediate recall on all of our meds. He seemed as upset and surprised as I was. Up until last night, I held out hope that he wasn't involved. When he called and told me about Greg, I was almost relieved. Then when Dr. Jarrell showed up and tried to take me, I felt so sick, so shattered. I'm still in shock because it means my instincts were right all along—and yet I went to *him* instead of you. And for that, I will never forgive myself."

He leaned close enough to see the sincerity in her

eyes. "You should be in shock. If you'd leveled with me to begin with I wouldn't have exposed you like I did out at the lake or last night in a glass room. I would have gotten you as far away from that man as possible. You worked with him every day, day in and day out. You could have been killed, Selena." He made a fist, holding it tight against his side. "And for *that,* I will never forgive *myself.*"

She reached out, her hand covering his. "I wasn't killed, Brice. I'm here, right here. And yes, I should have trusted you more. But what about you? When were you planning to trust me?"

He pulled away from her touch. "No, no. You will not turn the tables on me. I trusted you. I tried to trust you."

"You tried, but you doubted me, didn't you? You doubted me so much you set me up last night. And I'm not talking about being held at gunpoint. You set me up with typical Brice Whelan charm to fall for you and…I did. I did. Was that fair? You took my fears and my suspicions and…my feelings…and like a perfect CHAIM operative, you used them against me in the worst way. So you tell me, how is that any different from me withholding information from you?"

He couldn't answer that right now because her words had his gut all twisted up. And because right now, he wanted to kiss her instead of intimidate her. But he couldn't do that either. He had to finish the job.

So he leaned close, so close that he could smell her sweet perfume, and he said in a lethal whisper, "The difference, darlin', is that I was trying to save you. From yourself."

She stood back with a gasp, followed by a vivid flush of anger. "Brice—"

"We're done here," he said, disgusted with his sappy heart and with her sad attempts at explanations. "You've told me enough. You can give an official report to Shane and to all the other law enforcement agencies that will surely be called in on this case. Shane will be more objective on this than I was. After I explain things to your father, I'm removing myself from this case and I'm going back to Ireland." He turned his back to her to keep from begging her back into his arms. "You're free to go."

"You're wrong there," she said, her voice catching. "I'll never be completely free again."

He heard her intake of breath, heard her feet hitting the throw rug. Then he heard the door open and close as she left him standing there.

Minus his heart.

SIXTEEN

A week later Delton Carter sat across the breakfast table from Selena, his bushy eyebrows gathered in a solid frown of disapproval as he read the lengthy dossier on Dr. Henry Jarrell. With a grunt that mirrored the anger flashing in his eyes, he threw the file down and stared at Selena.

"I can't believe this."

"Neither could I," she said, her fingers feeling the warmth of her coffee cup. "It's so hard to imagine."

Delton grunted again. "We trusted him. He was a close friend. He helped deliver you when you were born—that's how highly we regarded him."

"I know, Daddy." She wished she could take away her father's pain and she also wished she could erase the constant burning agony inside her heart. "I think I became a nurse because of Dr. Jarrell. And I think he was once a good man. He just got caught up in greed and opportunity. He needed extra money and he found a way to obtain it."

"Yes, he certainly did, by setting up an underground factory in China so he could mass produce counterfeit drugs then have those drugs shipped to the clinic pharmacies, knowing that people could die from this. Not to mention the distribution center right here under our noses and the dangerous drugs he'd sold to who knows how many medical institutions. It's sickening, just sickening." He lifted his gaze to her. "And he almost killed you, Selena. He almost killed you."

Selena lowered her head, unable to finish her toast. She'd rehashed this a thousand times inside her mind. If she'd told Brice her suspicions from the very beginning, Vern wouldn't have gotten shot and Greg Gordon wouldn't be dead right now.

And she might be with Brice.

Brice. He had a certain code of honor and that code did not tolerate sins of omission or withholding information. It also didn't tolerate withholding feelings. She'd done both and she'd destroyed his heart in the process. And her own.

"Will we ever know how many patients actually died from this?" she asked her father, her heart heavy with the burden of that question. "I know this killed Mr. Cooper and I'm pretty sure we had several other patients die at the Haven Center Clinic due to this. But down in Día Belo we lost patients on a weekly basis for one reason or another. Now, I wonder if half of those patients died because they were taking placebos instead of real medication."

"We'll never have an exact number, honey," Delton said. "But I think you're right. Jarrell will spend a long time in jail for this, let me tell you. Brice and Shane have built a solid case and, with your testimony to the FDA, well, the man will live to regret his greed and trickery, that's for sure."

Selena got up to put her breakfast dishes in the sink. "I can't think about this anymore today. I'm going crazy. I need to get back to work."

"You can't," Delton needlessly reminded her. "Not until this entire investigation is over and you're clear."

"Then what am I supposed to do?" Selena asked. She'd been suspended from the clinic and from the hospital where she'd sometimes subbed for coworkers. Suspended until she was cleared to practice nursing again. Delton kept telling her it was just a precaution, just a necessary rule, but she knew no one trusted her right now—not to dispense or handle medication and certainly not to practice nursing. Because she had withheld evidence—even if her intentions had been good. No, make that misguided.

And she hated herself for that. Hated what this had done to her. She prayed minute by minute for God to show her the way and for Brice to give her another chance.

"Darling, let me do that."

Her mother hovered nearby, ready to fix everything. Selena didn't argue when Bea took over rinsing the dishes. She didn't have the strength. And she needed to be back in her apartment.

"I'm going home today," she said, her tone firm.

"But you are home," Bea countered, a mother's concern evident in her eyes. "You can stay here as long as you need to, honey."

Selena mustered up a smile. "I appreciate that, Mother, but I'm a big girl. I haven't been in my apartment for close to a month now and I want to go home."

Bea tossed a pleading glare at her husband. "Delton, are you listening? She wants to go back to her own place."

"I have ears, darlin'." He got up and stood across the massive granite counter, his gaze moving from his wife to his daughter. "Look, Selena, we just think you don't need to be alone right now. I mean, it's only been a few days since that lunatic held you at gunpoint. And it's only been a few days since—"

Her father stopped, his look changing from in control to helpless as he stared at his wife. "Well, you know."

"It's only been days since Brice went back to Ireland," Selena finished for her suddenly embarrassed father. "Yes, I'm well aware of that. But…I can't change any of this. I can't bring all those murdered people back, I can't do the work I love and…Brice is gone. He's gone and I don't blame him. I can't blame him. I just—"

It was her turn to stutter in humiliation. "I just can't find a way to forgive myself," she finally finished.

"Oh, my poor baby." Bea took Selena in her arms, hugging her close. "Brice will forgive you. He has to. He's just being a man—a CHAIM man. They don't like to admit defeat and they sure hate it when they can't crack a case."

"But it's my fault, Mother. I caused Brice so much trouble. It's all my fault."

Bea leaned back to put her hands on Selena's face. "Brice loves you. He'll be all right and you two will make up and things will be the way they were before."

"Things will never be the way they were before," Selena said, tears welling in her eyes. "Never."

Bea cut her gaze toward Delton. "Why don't you take that thick folder and go into your office, Del. Please?"

"Of course." Her father looked relieved to be away from all this feminine drama. He quickly gathered his briefcase and stalked out of the room.

"Now," Bea said, a smile centered on her face as she guided Selena back to her chair and sat down beside her. "What's this really all about? I understand that you're devastated about what Henry did, as we all are. But… this is about Brice, too, isn't it? You hurt him, but that hurt has not so much to do with withholding things as it does with being in love, am I right?"

Selena nodded, tears streaming down her face. "I withheld the most important thing of all, Mother. I held back my heart. I love him so much but I was too dumb to realize that until…until I almost died. And Brice could have been killed all because of me."

"Oh, honey," Bea said, taking Selena's hands in hers. "You love Brice, yes. Anyone can see that. But…it's not his forgiveness that you're seeking right now. First, you have to forgive yourself. Darling, you were frightened and confused and you were trying to protect a man you trusted and admired, a man you couldn't imagine doing anything so vile and evil. That has honor, whether you see that right now or not."

Selena got up, wiping at her eyes. "No, there is no honor in what I did. None at all."

"I think you're wrong there," Bea said. "I think the thing that has driven this wedge between you and Brice *is* your honor. You put that above your love for Brice. And now you have to find a way to show him that you care enough to give true honor to your love for him and for God."

"How do I do that, Mother?"

Bea shrugged. "You go to Brice and you tell him everything—and I mean everything—not anything more about this ugly business, but about this unfinished business between Brice and you. You tell him that you love him. This time, darling, you can't hold back."

"But how can I do that? I'm not sure I'm allowed to even leave the country."

Bea's soft grin widened. "You let me handle that. I've been a CHAIM wife for a long time. I know how to get things done. If you want to go to Ireland, then you'll be on the CHAIM jet within the hour—all perfectly legal and approved. You have my word on that. And it won't be against any kind of CHAIM or government regulations. Brice is an interrogator, after all. And you need interrogating, badly. It'll be part of this investigation. And a much better ending to this investigation, by my way of thinking."

Brice stood on the cliffs, watching the churning waters of the Atlantic Ocean below him while his gray stallion, Limerick, munched on some nearby grass. A fine mist of cool rain danced down on him from the sky, but he ignored the cold and the wet. He'd been with the dogs to the high country, searching for lost sheep. The two border collies, Greta and Piper, whimpered at his feet, probably wanting their supper after a day of hard work. Brice wasn't hungry and he wasn't inclined to head inside out of the rain either. He was bone weary, but he needed to be that way in order to sleep at night.

It was shearing season here on the farm and his one thousand acres covered the cliffs and the mountains but it wasn't nearly big enough for him to get away from his troubles.

He missed her.

He loved her.

He didn't think he could put one foot in front of the other and move another step without her. But Selena was thousands of miles away, across a vast ocean of water and wind and…regret.

He regretted how he'd treated her there toward the end. His mum had warned him that he was being too rash, just up and leaving like that. But he'd needed to get back here to the land he loved, to the place where he could find some sense of peace and spiritual strength.

So over the past week, he'd thrown himself into bringing the sheep down to be sheared, their fresh soft wool going into big bags to be shipped directly to the Whelan Wool factories and mills. He had the rest of the summer to keep himself busy with this hard, honest work. Work that would keep his mind off his mistakes and his longings. Work that made him tired. And yet, he couldn't sleep because he was afraid if he did, he'd dream of her in that green dress, dancing with him.

So he stood here, watching the water hitting the rocks and shore with an eternal, fierce anger and he felt that very same anger hitting at his heart, breaking it away piece by piece.

He should have forgiven her. He should have told her that he loved her above anything she might have done in the name of honor. He should have told her that she'd been right about him. He'd courted her for information, asking her to trust him, and all the while never once telling her that *he* trusted her. She'd sensed his distrust and that was the reason she'd been afraid to tell him her worst fears.

His failure was like a deep, jagged wound.

"Everyone feels his own wound first."

Brice thought of that old saying and nodded. Aye, he felt the wound, deep inside his heart. Would this love for her ever go away? Would this wound ever heal?

The dogs grew restless. Piper barked once, twice. Greta whimpered and moved in dainty circles around Brice's muddy black boots. Even the big stallion snorted and danced. "What's the matter with the lot of you?"

Then he turned around from the wind and the mist and saw her standing a few yards away, the backdrop of Whelan Castle framing her as if she was meant to be in just such a picture.

It took his breath away. And his anger.

The dogs reached her before he did and she leaned down, her golden-red hair falling in damp tendrils around her face and shoulders. She was wearing a dark rain cape and blue jeans and a soft, insecure smile.

"Hi," she said as he walked up the hill to her.

"Hi." He couldn't breathe. "How'd you get here?"

She tossed her hair away. "Permission from several law enforcement agencies, a CHAIM jet, a taxi from the airport, then a ride on a scooter from a kind neighbor."

He saw the tremble of her lips and felt it inside his heart. "Quite a trip."

She nodded, her eyes holding his. "Yes, it's taken a while for me to find my way."

He thought of a line from "The Planter's Daughter," a poem. "Oh, she was the Sunday in every week."

She slanted her head, her hand on Piper's fur. "How are you?"

He wasn't sure how to answer that question. Should he say miserable, unhappy, bitter and lonely? Or should he just answer "Fine"?

"Right now, I'm tired, smelly and wet," he said instead. "Let's get inside and make a cup of tea."

But her hand on his arm stopped that idea. "Brice, I need to talk to you."

An understatement.

"About what?"

Dumb question.

She glanced out at the clouds and water then looked back directly into his eyes. "About us." When he tried to form words, she shook her head. "Let me do the talking, okay?"

He nodded, afraid she'd take her arm away if he moved. And he needed that tiny spot of warmth.

"Remember what you told me when you first got involved in helping me? You said if the messenger is slow, go to meet him. Well, I'm here to meet you, Brice. I'm here and I'm asking you to forgive me—for not being honest with you, for not telling you the truth about Dr. Jarrell, about the pills, and about…how much I love you. I'm so sorry. If you can't be my friend anymore, I'll understand. But I can't bear any of this without you—without knowing you forgive me, Brice. I just can't. So…can you please forgive me?"

He looked up at the home he loved, thought about all the broken souls who'd come here, some seeking redemption, some hiding from the world, and some, just seeking, always seeking. And never finding. But this woman, she'd come halfway around the world. For him. And he owed her forgiveness. So much. Because he had failed her, so many times.

When he didn't answer right away, she said, "You also told me something else and I'm saying it to you now. You can't stay mad at me forever. Can you?"

Brice looked down at her hand on his arm, then he looked around, back out at the water. He ran a hand through his damp, windblown hair, let out a sigh, said a prayer, then without any more hesitation, he pulled her into his arms and held her tight, hugging her, his hands moving through her hair until he found her face. And then, he kissed her tears away, one by one, before his lips touched hers. When he finished kissing her, he pulled back to stare into her flower-blossom eyes. "You came here to find me then?"

"Of course," she said, smiling and crying at the same time. "But mostly, I came here so you could find me. The real me."

He liked the real her. "Do you plan on staying a bit?"

"I plan on staying as long as you want me here. My father pulled a lot of strings to get me into this retreat."

He nodded. "Did he now? I like the sound of that."

She looked up at him, her eyes devoid of any guilt or trickery. "Do you forgive me then?"

He was humbled by the sweetness of her words. "Nothing to forgive, luv, except my own stubborn pride. And the way I failed you."

"You didn't fail me, Brice. Never. Ever."

"But—"

"Can we just call it even? I'm not holding anything against you, even if you did charm me with your Irish ways."

"I'd say it's an even draw on that account, since you had me charmed from the first time I laid eyes on you."

"I did?"

"You did. When I saw you way back, I thought of a poem and I longed to hear you say the words in that poem."

She wiped at her eyes. "Of course, a poem. How appropriate. How did it go?"

He grinned, his taut jaw muscles hurting from the effort since he hadn't smiled in days. "It's by Padraic Colum: 'She put her arms 'round me; these words she did say: It will not be long, love, 'til our wedding day!'"

Her eyes grew as misty as the sky. "That's a very nice poem. Lovely."

"Does it make any sense?"

She leaned her head against his cheek. "It makes perfect sense if you're asking me to marry you."

He held her face between his hands. "Ach, that I am. Will you then?"

"I'd be honored."

The dogs barked and circled them. The stallion lifted his face to the wind and shook his long white mane. And the rain stopped. The sky to the west cleared to reveal puffy pink clouds and shards of brilliant golden light.

Brice pulled her around in front of him, pointing to the west as he leaned his chin against the top of her head. "Look at that sunset."

"We finally found it."

He turned her, kissed her once more for good

measure, then lifted her in his arms and carried her away, up to his castle.

And knew he'd found his shepherd's heart again.

Dear Reader,

Have you ever wanted to do the right thing but were afraid of the consequences? This is the dilemma that my hero and heroine in this book both faced. Brice knew he had to get Selena to safety, but he also knew that she'd resent him for doing his job. Couple that with the fact that he loved her and he had a real problem. Selena wanted to find out why the village where she was a beloved missionary had been attacked, but in her heart she had already figured out that someone close to her was probably to blame.

Both Brice and Selena brought long-held fears and secrets into their relationship. And that's exactly what we do with God sometimes. We know in our heart what is right and good and yet we're afraid to let go and trust that He will show us the way.

But the good news is that we don't have to hide our fears and secrets from God. He is willing to listen and give us unconditional love. Brice and Selena both learned this truth by slowly opening up to each other and their faith. I hope you enjoyed sharing this journey with them and maybe their story will help you with your own doubts and fears.

Until next time, may the angels watch over you. Always.

Lenora

QUESTIONS FOR DISCUSSION

1. Brice had a job to do but he also wanted Selena to forgive him for doing that job. Have you ever had to make a choice where your work caused someone else pain?

2. Selena was a true missionary, going to a foreign country to help others. What do you think it takes to do this? Have you ever wanted to work in a foreign country?

3. Why was it so difficult for Brice to interrogate Selena? Have you ever had to question a friend or loved one's motives?

4. Selena didn't know that Brice was in love with her. Do you think she would have treated him differently if she'd realized this?

5. Why did Selena try so hard to protect Dr. Jarrell? Have you ever felt someone you loved or respected might be doing something wrong?

6. It takes a lot of courage to be a nurse. Selena had to be strong just to get through the day. How do you find courage in your own work? Does your faith help?

7. Brice had a stable, loving home life in spite of his secretive career. Do you believe this helped him to overcome all his doubts and fears concerning Selena?

8. Selena resented Brice's job because her own father worked for the same secretive organization. Have you ever resented a loved one's work?

9. Why did Selena hold back from telling Brice everything she suspected? Do you believe she did the right thing in the end?

10. Why do you think Dr. Jarrell chose the path he took? How could he have handled things differently?

11. Selena cared about her parents. Do you think she cared too much? Do you believe her efforts showed her faith and Christianity?

12. Why was Brice so angry with Selena in the end? Do you think it had more to do with his personal feelings for her instead of the job he had to do? Or did it involve both? How can Christians today keep their personal feelings separate from their jobs, especially when a job might mean you see things you don't agree with?

*Turn the page for a sneak peek of
Shirlee McCoy's suspense-filled story,*
THE DEFENDER'S DUTY
*On sale in May 2009 from
Steeple Hill Love Inspired® Suspense.*

After weeks in intensive care, police officer Jude
Sinclair is finally recovering from the hit-and-run
accident that nearly cost him his life. But was it
an accident after all? Jude has his doubts—which
get stronger when he spots a familiar black car
outside his house: the same kind that accelerated
before running him down two months ago.
Whoever wants him dead hasn't given up, and
anyone close to Jude is in danger. Especially
Lacey Carmichael, the stubborn, beautiful home-
care aide who refuses to leave his side, even if it
means following him into danger....

"We don't have time for an argument," Jude said. "Take a look outside. What do you see?"

Lacey looked and shrugged. "The parking lot."

"Can you see your car?"

"Sure. It's parked under the streetlight. Why?"

"See the car to its left?"

"Yeah. It's a black sedan." Her heart skipped a beat as she said the words, and she leaned closer to the glass. "You don't think that's the same car you saw at the house tonight, do you?"

"I don't know, but I'm going to find out."

Lacey scooped up the grilled-cheese sandwich and shoved it into the carryout bag. "Let's go."

He eyed her for a moment, his jaw set, his gaze hot. "We're not going anywhere. You are staying here. I am going to talk to the driver of that car."

"I think we've been down this road before and I'm pretty sure we both know where it leads."

"It leads to you getting fired. Stay put until I get back, or forget about having a place of your own for a month." He stood and limped away, not even giving Lacey a second glance as he crossed the room and headed into the diner's kitchen area.

Probably heading for a back door.

Lacey gave him a one-minute head start and then

followed, the hair on the back of her neck standing on end and issuing a warning she couldn't ignore. Danger. It was somewhere close by again, and there was no way she was going to let Jude walk into it alone. If he fired her, so be it. As a matter of fact, if he fired her, it might be for the best. Jude wasn't the kind of client she was used to working for. Sure, there'd been other young men, but none of them had seemed quite as vital or alive as Jude. He didn't seem to need her, and Lacey didn't want to be where she wasn't needed. On the other hand, she'd felt absolutely certain moving to Lynchburg was what God wanted her to do.

"So, which is it, Lord? Right or wrong?" She whispered the words as she slipped into the diner's hot kitchen. A cook glared at her, but she ignored him. Until she knew for sure why God had brought her to Lynchburg, Lacey could only do what she'd been paid to do— make sure Jude was okay.

With that in mind, she crossed the room, heading for the exit and the client that she was sure was going to be a lot more trouble than she'd anticipated when she'd accepted the job.

Jude eased around the corner of the restaurant, the dark alleyway offering him perfect cover as he peered into the parking lot. The car he'd spotted through the window of the restaurant was still parked beside Lacey's. Black. Four door. Honda. It matched the one that had pulled up in front of his house, and the one that had run him down in New York.

He needed to get closer.

A soft sound came from behind him. A rustle of

fabric. A sigh of breath. Spring rain and wildflowers carried on the cold night air. Lacey.

Of course.

"I told you that you were going to be fired if you didn't stay where you were."

"Do you know how many times someone has threatened to fire me?"

"Based on what I've seen so far, a lot."

"Some of my clients fire me ten or twenty times a day."

"Then I guess I've got a ways to go." Jude reached back and grabbed her hand, pulling her up beside him.

"Is the car still there?"

"Yeah."

"Let me see." She squeezed in closer, her hair brushing his chin as she jockeyed for a better position.

Jude pulled her up short. Her wrist was warm beneath his hand. For a moment he was back in the restaurant, Lacey's creamy skin peeking out from under her dark sweater, white scars crisscrossing the tender flesh. She'd shoved her sleeve down too quickly for him to get a good look, but the glimpse he'd gotten was enough. There was a lot more to Lacey than met the eye. A lot she hid behind a quick smile and a quicker wit. She'd been hurt before, and he wouldn't let it happen again. No way was he going to drag her into danger. Not now. Not tomorrow. Not ever. As soon as they got back to the house, he was going to do exactly what he'd threatened—fire her.

"It's not the car." She said it with such authority, Jude stepped from the shadows and took a closer look.

"Why do you say that?"

"The one back at the house had tinted glass. Really dark. With this one, you can see in the back window. Looks like there is a couple sitting in the front seats. Unless you've got two people after you, I don't think that's the same car."

She was right.

Of course she was.

Jude could see inside the car, see the couple in the front seats. If he'd been thinking with his head instead of acting on the anger that had been simmering in his gut for months, he would have seen those things long before now. "You'd make a good detective, Lacey."

"You think so? Maybe I should make a career change. Give up home-care aide for something more dangerous and exciting." She laughed as she pulled away from his hold and stepped out into the parking lot, but there was tension in her shoulders and in the air. As if she sensed the danger that had been stalking Jude, felt it as clearly as Jude did.

"I'm not sure being a detective is as dangerous or as exciting as people think. Most days it's a lot of running into brick walls. Backing up, trying a new direction." He spoke as he led Lacey across the parking lot, his body still humming with adrenaline.

"That sounds like life to me. Running into brick walls, backing up and trying new directions."

"True, but in my job the brick walls happen every other day. In life, they're usually not as frequent." He waited while she got into her car, then closed the door, glancing in the black sedan as he walked past. An elderly woman smiled and waved at him, and Jude waved back, still irritated with himself for the mistake he'd made.

Now that he was closer, it was obvious the two cars he'd seen weren't the same. The one at his place had been sleeker and a little more sporty. Which proved that when a person wanted to see something badly enough, he did.

"That wasn't much of a meal for you. Sorry to cut things short for a false alarm." He glanced at Lacey as he got into the Mustang, and was surprised that her hand was shaking as she shoved the key into the ignition.

He put a hand on her forearm. "Are you okay?"

"Fine."

"For someone who is fine, your hands sure are shaking hard."

"How about we chalk it up to fatigue?"

"How about you admit you were scared?"

"Were? I still am." She started the car, and Jude let his hand fall away from her arm.

"You don't have to be. We're safe. For now."

"It's the 'for now' part that's got me worried. Who's trying to kill you, Jude? Why?"

"If I had the answers to those questions, we wouldn't be sitting here talking about it."

"You don't even have a suspect?"

"Lacey, I've got a dozen suspects. More. Every wife who's ever watched me cart her husband off to jail. Every son who's ever seen me put handcuffs on his dad. Every family member or friend who's sat through a murder trial and watched his loved one get convicted because of the evidence I put together."

"Have you made a list?"

"I've made a hundred lists. None of them have done me any good. Until the person responsible comes calling again, I've got no evidence, no clues and no way to link anyone to the hit and run."

"Maybe he won't come calling again. Maybe the hit and run was an accident, and maybe the sedan we saw outside your house was just someone who got lost and ended up in the wrong place." She sounded like she really wanted to believe it. He should let her. That's what he'd done with his family. Let them believe the hit and run was a fluke thing that had happened and was over. He'd done it to keep them safe. He'd do the opposite to keep Lacey from getting hurt.

* * * * *

*Will Jude manage to scare Lacey away, or will he
learn that the best way to keep her safe is to keep her
close...for as long as they both shall live?
To find out, read
THE DEFENDER'S DUTY
by Shirlee McCoy
Available May 2009
from Love Inspired Suspense*

REQUEST YOUR FREE BOOKS!

2 FREE RIVETING INSPIRATIONAL NOVELS
PLUS 2 FREE MYSTERY GIFTS

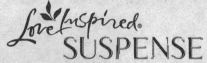

YES! Please send me 2 FREE Love Inspired® Suspense novels and my 2 FREE mystery gifts (gifts are worth about $10). After receiving them, if I don't wish to receive any more books, I can return the shipping statement marked "cancel". If I don't cancel, I will receive 4 brand-new novels every month and be billed just $4.24 per book in the U.S. or $4.74 per book in Canada, plus 25¢ shipping and handling per book and applicable taxes, if any*. That's a savings of over 20% off the cover price! I understand that accepting the 2 free books and gifts places me under no obligation to buy anything. I can always return a shipment and cancel at any time. Even if I never buy another book, the two free books and gifts are mine to keep forever.

123 IDN ERXX   323 IDN ERXM

Name	(PLEASE PRINT)
Address	Apt. #
City	State/Prov. Zip/Postal Code

Signature (if under 18, a parent or guardian must sign)

Order online at www.LoveInspiredSuspense.com
Or mail to Steeple Hill Reader Service:
IN U.S.A.: P.O. Box 1867, Buffalo, NY 14240-1867
IN CANADA: P.O. Box 609, Fort Erie, Ontario L2A 5X3

Not valid to current subscribers of Love Inspired Suspense books.

Want to try two free books from another series?
Call 1-800-873-8635 or visit www.morefreebooks.com

* Terms and prices subject to change without notice. N.Y. residents add applicable sales tax. Canadian residents will be charged applicable provincial taxes and GST. Offer not valid in Quebec. This offer is limited to one order per household. All orders subject to approval. Credit or debit balances in a customer's account(s) may be offset by any other outstanding balance owed by or to the customer. Please allow 4 to 6 weeks for delivery. Offer available while quantities last.

Your Privacy: Steeple Hill Books is committed to protecting your privacy. Our Privacy Policy is available online at www.SteepleHill.com or upon request from the Reader Service. From time to time we make our lists of customers available to reputable third parties who may have a product or service of interest to you. If you would prefer we not share your name and address, please check here. ☐

LISUS08R

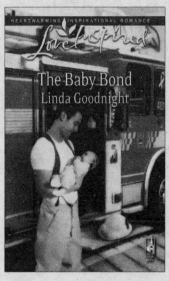

Firefighter Nic Carano relishes his bachelor lifestyle. Then he loses his heart to a rescued baby. And when he meets the infant's lovely aunt, Nic starts considering love, marriage…and a baby carriage. But after all Cassidy Willis has been through, she's not convinced she wants to spend her life with someone whose life is always in danger.

Look for

The Baby Bond

by

Linda Goodnight

Available May wherever books are sold.

Love Inspired ®
SUSPENSE

TITLES AVAILABLE NEXT MONTH

Available May 12, 2009

THE DEFENDER'S DUTY by Shirlee McCoy
The Sinclair Brothers

Recuperating cop Jude Sinclair doesn't want anyone
near him—especially not beautiful health aide
Lacey Carmichael. His attacker *will* be back.
And anyone close to him is at risk....

DEADLY COMPETITION by Roxanne Rustand
Without a Trace

The single mother is still missing, and her daughter needs
more care than her uncle, Clint Herald, knows how to give.
Nanny Mandy Erick steps in so capably that Clint enters
her in a Mother of the Year contest. With Mandy's secrets,
though, attention could be deadly.

PROTECTING HER CHILD by Debby Giusti
Magnolia Medical

Before she dies, wealthy heiress Eve Townsend must find
the daughter she gave up for adoption. Medical researcher
Pete Worth is ready to find answers. Instead, he uncovers
more questions when he finds Meredith Lassiter widowed,
pregnant—and on the run.

THE TAKING OF CARLY BRADFORD by Ramona Richards
When Dee Kelley finds a pair of child's sandals in the woods,
she's determined to help find the missing girl. Nothing police
chief Tyler Madison says can dissuade her. But Tyler isn't
the only one who wants her off the case. And it's not just
evidence awaiting Dee in the woods.